Ceci Jenkinson lives in Wales with her husband, two sons (who give her lots of ideas for the Oli and Skipjack stories) and two border terriers (who keep her company while she writes - and pinch her biscuits whenever she stops to gaze out of the window).

The Mum Shop was shortlisted for the Sheffield Children's Book Award 2009 and *Gnomes Are Forever* was shortlisted for Waterstone's Children's Book Prize 2009.

For more about Oli and Skipjack go to:

www.cecijenkinson.net

Praise for Oli and Skipjack's Tales of Trouble:

'Oli and Skipjack have all the makings of
a classic pairing . . . Ceci Jenkinson has an
instinctive feel for her audience and writes with
pace and humour.' *Daily Telegraph*

'Jenkinson's style is quirky and extremely funny
and the pacing is brilliant. [*Gnomes are Forever*]
quickly becomes impossible to put down.' *Irish
News*

'A marvellously funny book. An array of weird
and wacky characters – complete with weird and
wacky gadgets – makes [*The Spookoscope*] a great
book that both boys and girls will absolutely
love.' *Waterstone's Books Quarterly*

'I rated [*The Mum Shop*] 10/10 because it was a
brilliant book.' Elizabeth Rhodes, age 11

'It's fantastic! *The Mum Shop* gets my vote for the
best book.' Kennedy Tookey, age 10

'I definitely give [*The Mum Shop*] 5 stars.'
Charlotte-Grace Oxley, age 11

MIRROR MISCHIEF

CECI JENKINSON

Illustrations by
Michael Broad

faber and faber

First published in 2010
by Faber and Faber Limited
Bloomsbury House, 74–77 Great Russell Street,
London, WC1B 3DA

Typeset by Mandy Norman
Printed in England by CPI BookMarque, Croydon

A CIP record for this book
is available from the British Library

ISBN 978-0-571-24969-5

2 4 6 8 10 9 7 5 3

For Ian and Jill, Jee, Sa and Arthur,
Daniel and Olivia and
the barefoot bottoms

CONTENTS

1   A Parcel of Surprises   1

2   Double Trouble for Oli   12

3   Revolting Reflections   28

4   Blue Bottom Horror   40

5   Scary Hairy Slugger   53

6   A Smashing Time   66

7   Monkey Business   78

8   Zomu's Spell   92

9   The Curse of the Uncursed   103

10 Zombies and Cannibals   113

11 Eyeballs, Teeth and Toenails   123

12 Showdown with Mr Surd   134

13 Loose Ends   149

1
A Parcel of Surprises

At 7.27 precisely on Monday morning, the alarm clock beside Mr Vernon Surd's narrow iron bed began to ring. Mr Surd reached out a long bony arm and flicked it off. He always set his alarm for 7.27, as this allowed him a lie-in of exactly three minutes. Any longer would have been lazy, and Mr Surd frowned on laziness. In fact, Mr Surd frowned on almost everything.

Mondays always started with Double Maths for Year 7. Mr Surd's hands clenched into knots under the coverlet and he frowned his frowniest frown. All the children he tried to teach were stupid but Year 7 had not a single brain between them. Their refusal to grasp fractions was so stubborn that he sometimes suspected them of pretending not to understand, just to irritate him.

When his allotted 180 seconds were up, Mr Surd climbed out of his creaky bed and drew back his thin curtains. His dark mood grew even darker when he saw the cloudless blue sky outside and the early-morning sunlight already glowing on the rooftops. He hated sunny days. Sunny days made children gaze out of the window and wish they were playing outside. He would have to keep Year 7 extra busy today.

At 7.30 a.m. Mrs Stubbins went to the foot of the stairs, took a deep breath and hollered 'MELVYN!' at top volume, startling the birds from the trees and causing old Mrs Higginbottom next door to fall out of bed. But her son, commonly known as Slugger, merely grunted under his duvet and rolled over.

At 7.40 a.m., Mrs Stubbins marched into Slugger's room, yelled, 'MELVYN!' again and pulled all the covers off the bed, revealing what appeared to be a young hippopotamus underneath. Yawning and scratching, Slugger hauled his large and lumpy body out of bed. As his tiny brain slowly woke up, he began to wonder what amusements the day would provide. He could start by taking the junior boys' lunch money as usual. After that he could bully Nerdy Ned about his stutter. A broad grin spread over Slugger's

flabby face at the prospect of all this fun. Then he thought of someone else: Oli Biggles. He scowled.

At 7.45 a.m., eleven-year-old Oli Biggles was snatching a few final seconds in his cosy bed and re-living a beautiful moment from yesterday's rugby practice. He was running with the ball and he neatly sidestepped a diving tackle from Slugger Stubbins, whom he left grabbing armfuls of thin air while he whizzed on to score a try between the posts.

Slugger was still face down in the mud – by far the best place for him – when Oli's younger sister Tara marched into his bedroom to announce that if he wasn't downstairs in five minutes Mum would eat his waffles. Electrified by this terrible threat, Oli sprang from his bed, scrambled into his clothes and shot down to the kitchen with just ten seconds to spare.

Tara was already tucking into her waffles and at the far end of the table sat Oli's other sister Becky, nibbling a grape. Becky was fourteen and, in Oli's opinion, the most boring person ever invented. Becky would no doubt have thought the same of Oli, if she had bothered to think of him at all.

Waffle Breakfast had become a Monday morning treat in the Biggles house, a moment of maple syrup and happiness to fend off Oli's fear of Double Maths. This morning the waffles' job of providing cheer was helped by a bulky parcel which sat beside Oli's plate. Parcels are always exciting and this one was almost entirely covered in exotic stamps, with just a small space for Oli's name and address in the middle.

'It's from Sid!' cried Oli in delight. Sid ran the local pizza shop, where she made the best triple-pepperoni pizzas in town. She was large and jolly with curly orange hair and she had helped Oli and his best friend Skipjack out of many narrow scrapes.

'She's been on holiday for ages,' remarked Tara. 'Where is she now?'

Oli tore the parcel open at one end and drew out a postcard. It showed a smiling African man standing in front of a thatched hut. The man's smile was surprising given his circumstances: he was entirely festooned with pythons. Pythons were coiled around his neck and hung in thick ropes from his outstretched arms. Intrigued by this human snake-tidy, Oli turned the postcard over.

'She sent this from a snake temple in Benin,' he said, reading the back. 'It must have taken ages to get here, cos she's coming back on Wednesday.'

'Benin!' exclaimed Tara. 'That's so unfair – I've been saving up for years to go to Africa.'

Oli reached into the parcel and pulled out a large wooden object.

'It's a mirror – cool!'

'It's beautiful,' said Mum. 'Look at those carved animals around the frame.'

Tara announced, 'They're chameleons. They give you the Evil Eye.'

'Not that you'd need one of those,' remarked Oli, 'having two already.'

'I wish I did,' retorted Tara. 'I could double curse you.'

Oli read Sid's postcard. 'It's to both of us. Listen: "Hiya Oli and Tara! I'm having a smashing time here in Africa. I bought these from a groovy medicine man. He says they have Magic Powers! Must go or I'll miss the bus to Burkina Faso. Lots of love, Sid."'

'So there's a present for me as well!' cried Tara. She grabbed the envelope, felt about inside and pulled out a small brown leather bag, tied at the neck with beaded strings. She loosened the strings and shook the contents of the bag onto the table.

Everyone stared down at a pile of tiny white bones.

'Fortune-telling bones!' exclaimed Tara. 'I know all about these –'

'Of course you do,' muttered Oli, rolling his eyes.

'You cast them on the ground,' Tara continued, 'and then you look at the pattern they fall in and that tells you about the future.'

Oli peered at the bones. 'I wonder what they're saying now,' he said.

'I can tell you exactly what they're saying,' said Mum.

'You can?' chorused her children, impressed.

'Yes. They're telling you that if you don't get a move on you'll be late for school.'

Excitement of an entirely different kind was approaching Mr Vernon Surd as he stood at the bus stop with his eyes peeled for the Number 11. Ah, here she came and yes – she was indeed completely re-painted! Mr Surd had looked forward to this moment for months, ever since he had read about the plan for new colours in his favourite magazine *Bus-Spotters' Monthly*. Now, brimming with emotion, Mr Surd clutched his briefcase a little tighter and for a fleeting second he looked almost happy.

The gleaming bus arrived and Mr Surd drew an approving finger along the smooth red paintwork before boarding. 'What a marvellous job they've done on your bus, Mr Grimble!' he said to the driver. 'You must be a very proud man.'

'It makes a change from driving a rusty old heap,' agreed Mr Grimble, in an unusually cheerful mood.

'I shall have to bring my camera tomorrow,' said Mr Surd. 'I should like a photograph of her smart new paintwork for my collection.'

'If only everybody respected my bus like you, Mr Surd,' commented Mr Grimble and then he clenched his teeth, for he had just spotted through his rear-view mirror a pair of the most disrespectful bodies on the planet. They were cycling along behind him and, as he drew up at a red light, they manoeuvred their bikes through the narrow space between the kerb and his beautiful red bus.

'If they get so much as one tiny scratch on my

nice new paintwork I'll run them over,' growled
the bus driver.

The two cyclists risking Death By Number
11 Bus were in fact Oli Biggles and his best
friend Skipjack Haynes on their way to school.
They were followed by Tara, at the distance she
always kept when she wanted to pretend she had
nothing to do with them.

'Look, Skip – a new Number 11,' shouted Oli.

'Let's hope it's got a new driver,' Skipjack

shouted back. He reached the front of the bus, peered in and saw the familiar, extravagantly hairy face of Mr Grimble glaring back at him. 'No such luck. Hello, Mr Grimble. What colour are they going to paint you?'

'Come on, Skip – the light's green,' called Oli. 'Bye, Mr Grimble!'

'Bet you can't catch up!' yelled Skipjack over his shoulder and the boys sped off, leaving Mr Grimble muttering through his beard.

2 Double Trouble for Oli

'So, Skip,' panted Oli as they pedalled along, 'Tell me more about the mask Sid sent you.'

'Well, she called it a Death Mask and it's made of some kind of bark. It's got a face painted on it with real live teeth and hair from a real live dead body. It's seriously ugly, Oli. I mean, if you put that mask and Slugger Stubbins side by side, you wouldn't be able to tell which was which.'

'I suppose it's got Magic Powers like my mirror?'

'Of course. I hope they're useful magic powers, like granting wishes or something.'

Oli said in a dreamy voice, 'Maybe I could wish to be brilliant at maths.'

Skipjack shook his head. 'You don't want to waste your wishes on maths,' he advised. 'And definitely not until you know how many you've got. Anyway, I've thought up a new way to get really good marks in maths. I call it my Theory of One. I'm going to try it out today.'

'How does it work?'

'Like this. I've noticed that when I get sums wrong, it's usually just by one number. So if I add one to whatever number I get at the end of a sum, or take one away, I'll end up with the right answer.'

'But how will you know whether to add one or take one away?'

'That's the tricky bit,' admitted Skipjack. 'I'll have to do "eeny, meeny, miney, mo". But at least I'll have a 50 per cent chance of getting it right rather than a 100 per cent chance of getting it wrong.'

Oli frowned. Something wasn't right about Skipjack's Theory of One but he could not quite put his finger on it.

While Oli was trying to pin down this slippery mathematical problem, Slugger Stubbins was beginning his morning dinner-money round.

Astronomers tell us that the gas giant Jupiter is orbited by sixteen moons. The gas giant Slugger had to make do with only four or five moons, round, blotchy-faced boys who followed him everywhere. After Slugger had spent a profitable fifteen minutes forcing cash out of several tiny victims who would now have to miss lunch, he turned his attention to Ned Trotter.

'Hello, N-N-N-Ned,' began Slugger mockingly. 'H-h-how are y-y-you?' The moons snorted with laughter.

Ned looked up from his computer magazine and blinked through his glasses. 'Oh, hello, S-Slugger,' he stammered.

Slugger shook his head sadly. 'Now, Ned, I don't remember ever giving you permission to call me that,' he said. 'Only cool people are allowed to call me Slugger. You aren't a cool person, are you, Ned?'

'Er, n-no, Slug- s-sorry, n-no.'

Slugger continued. 'So you have to call me Lord Stubbins. Understand, N-n-ned?'

'Yes, Slug – Lord Stubbins.'

The moons sniggered.

'I will now have to punish you for calling me Slugger, Ned. I hope this will help you learn the error of your ways.'

With these words he took the computer
magazine from Ned's thin hands and tore it into
little pieces. Then, to howls of laughter from his
fan club, he threw the shreds up in the air.

Oli and Skipjack arrived in the playground just in time to see Slugger and his sidekicks strolling away from Ned and the fluttering magazine confetti.

'What's he done this time, Ned?' asked Oli as they went over to help him pick up the pieces.

'H-he tore up my magazine,' mumbled Ned. 'There was a competition in it I wanted to enter.'

'Never mind,' said Skipjack. 'You just need to find the bits and stick them back together.'

Oli said, 'You really must learn to stick up for yourself more, Ned. You shouldn't make it this easy for Slugger to bully you.'

'N-Normally it doesn't b-bother me much,' said Ned. 'I'm n-not really worth sticking up for, if you know what I mean.'

'No, I don't,' said Oli.

'It's different for boys like you and Skipjack,' explained Ned, going red. 'But it doesn't matter if Slugger picks on me, cos everyone thinks I'm a nerd anyway.'

'That's not true,' protested both Oli and Skipjack. 'You aren't a nerd,' added Oli. 'You're a . . . a . . .'

He shot Skipjack a desperate glance.

'A boffin,' finished Skipjack. 'Which is quite different.'

Ned did not look convinced. 'In any c-case,' he said,'there's n-nothing I can do about Slugger, so it's best not to mind.'

'That's only because he's built like a rhino and you're such a –' Oli paused, '– and you're not. You need building up, Ned. You should join our rugby team.'

Skipjack winced. Much as he wanted Ned to build himself up, he didn't want it enough to risk losing all their matches. This thought must have occurred to Oli, too, for when Ned exclaimed, 'I couldn't p-possibly. Rugby is m-much too violent,' Oli made no attempt to persuade him. Instead he said, 'Well, we must think of something else to scare Slugger off.'

'Perhaps Ned could learn a war dance, like the Haka,' suggested Skipjack. 'It works for the All Blacks.'

'But the All Blacks don't look like a bunch of stick insects,' Oli pointed out. 'Sorry Ned.'

'That's true,' agreed Skipjack. 'Ah, well. I'm

going to see if Katie Adams has left any sweets in my desk.'

Oli looked surprised. 'I thought it was Nicky Jones?'

'That was last week. Try and keep up, Oli.'

Oli shook his head in wonder. 'What do they all see in you, Skip?'

'It's my big brown eyes,' Skipjack told him, opening them very wide. 'See? Girls love big brown eyes.' And he ran off, full of hope.

Oli picked up the last pieces of magazine. 'Don't forget, Ned,' he said as he handed them over, 'You must stand up to Slugger.'

Just then a huge shadow fell across them both.

'Oi, Biggles,' said a menacing voice.

Uh-oh, thought Oli. Me and my big mouth.

'I said, Oi, Biggles,' repeated the voice.

Oli rose slowly to stand up to Slugger.

'The name's Oli, Slugger, not "Oi",' he said smoothly. 'You forgot the "l". I know you find spelling difficult, Slugger, especially long words like "Oli", but you could at least try.'

While these words sank slowly through the thick crust of Slugger's brain, Ned gazed at Oli, awestruck. And, fuelled by his admiration, Oli pushed his luck.

'Did you enjoy your little mud bath on the rugby pitch yesterday, Slugger?' he enquired.

Slugger's eyes narrowed. 'That's what I want to talk to you about, Biggles. You were very quick, weren't you? But you made me look stupid. I don't like people who make me look stupid.'

'It must be terrible not to like yourself,' sighed Oli.

'I can be quick, too,' continued Slugger. 'Shall I show you how quick I can be?' And, after a glance to check that no teachers were watching, he shot his huge fist forwards and punched Oli hard in the stomach. Oli buckled like a tin can, while Slugger threw back his head in a loud guffaw. 'See?' he sneered, and he swaggered away.

Ned gazed at Oli, shock-struck. 'Are – are you OK, Oli?' he asked.

'Not really, no,' gasped Oli, still bent double and clutching his stomach. 'But that isn't important. The important thing is that I stood up to him.'

Ned frowned. 'I-I know this is going to disappoint you, Oli, but if that's what you get for standing up to Slugger, then I'd rather go on not standing up to him.'

It was to be a morning of mental as well as physical pain for Oli, as ten minutes later he was lowering his aching body into his seat for Double Maths.

'What happened to you?' asked Skipjack.

Oli told him and Skipjack shook his head. 'You really mustn't try to stand up for yourself, Oli. You should use my two tried-and-tested Anti-Slugger Tactics. I'll remind you what they are. Tactic 1: Drop to the ground, hug Slugger's knees and beg loudly for mercy. Slugger gets embarrassed, shakes you off his leg and walks away in disgust. Tactic 2 (my personal favourite): Run away.'

'Where's your pride, Skip?'

'Hiding under the bed.'

At the front of the classroom a hunched, black figure stood staring out of the window. This was the maths teacher Mr Vernon Surd. He held his hands behind his back and in one hand was a tapered stick about the length of a ruler, for pointing at sums on the board or pupils in the class. Skipjack claimed he had also seen Mr Surd pick his nose with this tool, but had been unable to produce the evidence. Mr Surd certainly possessed an enormous nose, whose deeper nooks and crannies would have been well beyond the reach of a normal human finger.

On the whiteboard was written one word: FRACTIONS. Oli's heart sank. Maths was bad enough with whole numbers, but when they started dividing themselves up willy-nilly it became impossible. They had spent the whole of last week on fractions and he had been no wiser by Friday.

Even his mum had tried to help. Think of pizza, she had said to him and Skipjack over lunch on Saturday. If you have three-quarters of one triple-pepperoni pizza and you add one third of another triple-pepperoni pizza, how much triple-pepperoni pizza do you get? But Oli had answered, 'Still not enough, especially with Skipjack around,' which only two thirds of them

had thought was very funny.

Mr Surd turned around slowly and glared at the class over his spectacles. 'Good morning, class,' he said in the usual Dalek voice that always made Oli hear 'Exterminate'. 'Last week,' continued Mr Surd, 'you failed to grasp even the basics of fractions, so we will start again today with addition. We will proceed to subtraction, multiplication and division of fractions. Tomorrow you will have a test. You each have a sheet of ten problems. Begin now.'

Oli looked at the little numbers on his sheet. Should he add the ones on top or the ones on the bottom? Or both? Or the top to the bottom? He stared blindly at the factions until they began to shimmer like a mirage, at which point he shook himself and looked up to see whether the rest of the class were steaming ahead or were, like him, baffled. Ned, of course, was steaming and for the first time in his life Oli almost wished he was a boffin. Skipjack was busy drawing pizzas with missing wedges. Slugger was craning his thick neck over Ned's thin shoulder and copying down his answers.

Mr Surd circled the desks. He walked with a limp, due to his right leg being slightly shorter than his left. Oli and Skipjack believed this was because his right leg was the one he used for stamping whenever he became irritated. And, as he became irritated several times a day, his poor leg was simply wearing down.

Mr Surd swooped down on Oli and picked up his paper.

'Oliver Biggles, you have failed to attempt even one sum.'

There was no denying this. 'Yes, sir,' said Oli.

'Let me guess: you have no idea how to add fractions.'

There was no denying this, either. 'No, sir,' said Oli.

'So everything that I went to such pains to teach you last week simply went straight over your head.'

'It looks like it, sir,' agreed Oli.

'Surely you know the answer to the first question?' demanded Mr Surd. 'What is the common denominator for 3 and 4? Well? Speak up – what is it?'

Oli knew he knew this, but his brain had shut down completely under Mr Surd's impatient glare. Come on, brain, he urged, but nothing happened. Several silent seconds ticked by until finally Mr Surd muttered with a shudder, 'Oliver Biggles, you are without question the stupidest boy I have ever had the extreme displeasure to teach.' He swept over to Slugger's desk and peered down at his paper. 'Even Stubbins here has completed several sums and, I might add, completed them correctly.'

Slugger shot Oli a look so stuffed with triumph that it seemed to come with its own trumpet blast. This was too much for Oli. Giving up all hope of surviving this most horrible of days with mind and body intact, he muttered, 'What a genius he must be, sir.'

Mr Surd froze. Then he marched to Oli's desk, raised his hand and whacked his pointed stick hard on the edge of the wood. Oli jumped.

'Thank you, Biggles,' whispered Mr Surd, 'but I'll provide the sarcasm.'

When at long last the lesson was over Oli caught hold of Ned in the corridor and whispered, 'Ned, Slugger was copying your answers!'

Ned nodded. 'I-I-I know, Oli. He always does. He says if I don't let him he'll make life nasty for my little brother in Year 2. I c-can't let that happen.'

Oli knew the little brother in question. He was a tiny replica of Ned, so small and skinny that Slugger could probably squash him between finger and thumb.

'Anyway,' continued Ned. 'It doesn't matter if he copies. It doesn't make my m-marks worse.'

'That's not the point!' exclaimed Oli. 'He's cheating. And he's using you. Where's your pride, Ned?'

'I c-can't afford to be proud, Oli,' said Ned. 'I have to be practical.'

At lunchtime Oli was still feeling sore. 'I think Slugger punched a hole right into my stomach,' he complained to Skipjack.

'Try some lunch,' suggested his friend helpfully. 'If it comes oozing out again, we'll know you leak.'

'I don't want to eat,' groaned Oli. 'Too

painful.'

While Skipjack tried to imagine not wanting to eat, and failed, Oli continued, 'I don't know who I hate more at the moment: Slugger or Mr Surd.'

'There's not much between them,' agreed Skipjack, eyeing Oli's lunch. 'But why do you have to choose? Can't you just hate them both the same?'

'Good idea,' agreed Oli, 'I hereby hate Slugger and Mr Surd with all the hate in Hateland.'

'Shame to let your lunch go to waste,' remarked Skipjack.

'I feel better now,' said Oli. 'I think I'll eat it after all.'

Skipjack sighed.

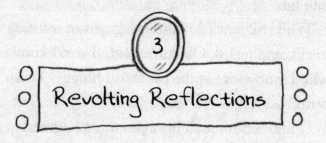

Revolting Reflections

At 7.27 precisely on Tuesday morning, the alarm clock beside Mr Vernon Surd's narrow iron bed began to ring. Mr Surd reached out a long, bony arm and flicked it off.

This was the day of the Fractions Test for Year 7. Vernon Surd frowned and chewed his thin lips. What punishment could he give to the ones who failed?

At about 7.40 a.m., Slugger was once again brought to life by the removal of his blankets and, as soon as thought was possible, put his mind to more playground fun and games.

At 7.45 a.m. Oli tried very hard not to wake up but a vision of Slugger barged into his brain with a swarming army of fractions and, by the time he had driven these invaders out, he was well and truly awake. He opened his eyes a tiny crack and saw his new mirror, propped up on his bedside table. He looked at the chameleons that were carved into the frame with curled-up tails and long, flicking tongues. He sat up and reached out for the mirror and then, holding it in both hands, he frowned into the glass.

Tara burst into his room, waving her bag of fortune-telling bones.

'These are amazing!' she cried.

'Shh, I'm concentrating.'

'Well, if you'd rather gaze at yourself than hear something amazing,' sniffed his sister, 'I'll go.'

'I'm not gazing at myself – I'm casting a spell on Slugger and Mr Surd.'

'I'm lucky. I don't have Mr Surd for maths. I have Miss Green and she's really nice. I'm good at maths. What kind of spell are you casting?'

'A spell to make them disappear for ever,' replied Oli through gritted teeth.

'Can you add Amelia Parker to your list? She was mean to me in netball yesterday.'

'No, I can't add Amelia Parker to my list. Put her on your own list.' Oli replaced the mirror on the bedside table and climbed out of bed.

'I haven't got a list,' said Tara. 'My bones can't make people disappear. They can only read the future.'

'So what's the amazing thing they told you?' asked Oli.

'Well, yesterday I asked them if I'd have a good day and they said, "not very". And I didn't have a very good day. Because of Amelia Parker and because of only getting 18 out of 20 in my French test.'

'So?'

'So, they told the truth!'

Oli rolled his eyes. 'It's not very specific, is it? I mean, it's not as if they told you that Amelia Parker would be mean to you in netball.'

Tara stuck her chin out. 'What about this, then: just now I asked them if I had any letters and they said "no" and I went downstairs to look and guess what?'

'You didn't have any letters,' sighed Oli.

'See?' Tara was triumphant.

'But you only get letters about twice a year.'

'That's not the point,' insisted Tara. 'I think you're just jealous.'

'Why don't you ask the bones if I am?'

All his sister could say to that was, 'Huh!' so she said it, and left.

Oli had one last look at his mirror before he went downstairs. If only it really did have magic powers.

The hour of the maths test arrived all too soon. Watching the stooping Mr Surd placing the papers on each desk, Oli was struck for the hundredth time by how repulsive his maths teacher was, with his black strands of greasy hair, sunken eyes and sallow face. He glanced from Mr Surd to Slugger, who was rocking back and forth on his chair, using his ruler to flick balls of paper at the back of Ned's head. He remembered his spell to make them disappear. If only.

He couldn't answer any of the questions in the test. His brain was still closed for business, with a sign on the door saying 'Back When Mr Surd Has Disappeared'. In the end he used Skipjack's Theory of One for some of the questions and, when he got tired of that, he used rugby scores from Wales's matches in the last Six Nations competition.

He was just gazing into space, trying to remember whether the result against France had been 34:12 or 37:12, when he caught sight of Slugger peering once again over Ned's shoulder. Ned had finished the test and appeared to be setting himself more problems at the bottom of his answer sheet, just for fun. As Oli watched, Slugger threw down his pencil, leaned back and gave a yawn that could have swallowed Australia. Then he scratched his armpit and picked up his pencil again to pick something out of a back tooth. Oli thought of his spell again. If only.

At last the break bell went and the children streamed out of the classroom. Oli and Skipjack found a corner of the playground where they could pass a ball back and forth and forget all about fractions.

Mr Surd went to the staff bathroom. As he washed his hands he looked in the mirror and noticed that his bald patch, normally concealed beneath carefully combed, oily strands of hair, was showing rather prominently. He put his hands to his head and was relieved to feel that the carefully combed hairs were still in place. He decided that the appearance of the bald patch in his reflection was probably just a smear on the glass.

Slugger went to the loo in the boys' changing rooms. He did not wash his hands. He did not look in the mirror.

Mr Surd went to the bathroom again at the beginning of lunch, not because he needed

to but because he believed in Always Going
When You Have the Opportunity. As he looked
in the mirror he was surprised to see that the
bald patch was still there and also that his nose
appeared longer. He felt his head and his nose.
Both seemed just as they always were. He stared
in the mirror again. Perhaps it contained a slight
bend which was distorting his reflection. He tried
a different mirror but the strange bald patch and
the long, hooked nose were still there. Slightly
disturbed, Mr Surd went outside for playground
duty.

Slugger went to the bathroom, too, not because he needed to but because he wanted to put cling film over the loo seat in cubicle 1. He then spent ten minutes waiting in cubicle 2 for a victim. He was rewarded for his patience by the arrival of the unsuspecting Nevis Bullionburger, who attempted to do what he had come to do and received a very nasty shock. Doubled up with laughter, Slugger staggered out of the changing rooms to tell everyone in the playground about Nevis's misfortune. He did not look in the mirror.

After a satisfying stint on playground duty (which produced three shoutings and a detention), Mr Surd returned to the bathroom once more to check on the mysterious bald patch. It was still there, together with the hooked nose, and now his eyes were looking strangely yellow and his skin had turned a rather worrying shade of grey. Perhaps I'm ill, thought Mr Surd. He put his hand up to his forehead to check his temperature and was very disturbed indeed to see that his fingers in the mirror were long and claw-like. He looked down at his hands. They were completely normal. I'm seeing things, he told himself. It's stress, that's what it is, caused by all those revolting children who refuse to understand fractions.

Slugger also went to the bathroom at the end of lunch. He did not wash his hands. He did not look in the mirror. He hung around for a while in the corridor to miss as much of the geography lesson as he dared and finally sauntered into the classroom fifteen minutes late.

'And just where have you been, Melvyn?' enquired Miss Green.

'I was abducted by aliens, miss. They took me up into their spaceship and wouldn't let me go.'

'How fascinating, Melvyn,' said Miss Green sweetly. 'Did you travel far in their spaceship?'

'Right round the world, miss,' said Slugger cockily.

'What a pity they couldn't take you even further,' commented Miss Green.

Throughout his afternoon lessons, Mr Surd was nervous and distracted. He kept feeling all over his head, as if checking that it had not fallen off, and examining his hands, as if he had never seen them before. He would glare furiously at anyone who so much as glanced at him. He forgot what he was saying, his words dribbling into long, empty silences. Even those who had long ago decided he was a complete odd-ball were newly struck by the extent of his odd-ballity.

Thankfully his last lesson was a free period, so he was finally able to retreat to the staff bathroom. He pushed open the door and went inside. Hardly daring to look, he kept his eyes on the floor as he approached the mirror. One, two, three . . .

Mr Surd looked up.

He saw a vulture.

Vernon Surd reeled back in horror, clutching his face. It couldn't be true! He looked down at himself. He was normal. He looked in the mirror. He was a vulture.

Then he heard footsteps approaching. Before anyone else could see the dreadful image, Mr Surd rushed out of the bathroom with a sheaf of papers held up to his face. But while this barrier concealed him from other people in the corridor, it also concealed other people in the corridor from him. Moments later someone came hurtling out of a side door and there was a head-on collision. Papers flew everywhere and Mr Surd landed with a bump on his bottom.

Skipjack, for he had been the side-door hurtler, braced himself for a Shouting. But Mr Surd was far too appalled at the prospect of being spotted to shout. Silent and cowering, he scrabbled his papers together while Skipjack, mystified by the teacher's bizarre behaviour, took his chance and fled.

Five minutes before the end of the last lesson, Slugger asked to be excused. After the phenomenal success of his Cling Film Trick at lunchtime, he wanted time to set up similar traps in the remaining loos before the other boys arrived to change for football practice.

With the roll of cling film up his sleeve he hurried back to the changing rooms. He was just stretching his invisible weapon over the last bowl when the bell rang for the end of school. Seconds later he heard the rest of the football club stampeding down the corridor. 'This will be immense,' chuckled Slugger as he nipped away from the loos, and he looked in the mirror to enjoy his brilliant reflection.

Looking back was a blue-faced baboon.

4

Blue Bottom Horror

The changing room doors crashed open and
a crowd of boys surged in. Slugger dived for
the floor. Hiding his head in his arms and bent
double to stay below the mirrors, he staggered
towards the nearest cubicle, slammed the bolt
home and leant against the door. His heart was
pounding so hard against his ribs that he felt as if
he had swallowed a prize boxer. He was going to
pass out. He was going to have a heart attack. He
was going to die.

There were bangs on the door. 'Why are you
hiding, Slugger?'

'He's shy, poor Slugger. He never realised how
ugly he was.'

With trembling fingertips, Slugger felt his
face. It seemed completely normal. He looked
down at his hands. They were normal, too. So

he hadn't turned into a blue-faced baboon. He began to calm down. Perhaps he wouldn't die, after all.

Scientists have declared that the animal with the smallest brain in relation to body size was the stegosaurus, but those scientists have overlooked the modern-day descendant of that Jurassic monster, namely Sluggersaurus, whose brain was as tiny as a peanut.

Positive now that the hideous image in the mirror had been merely a trick of the light or a figment of his imagination, Slugger came out of his cubicle. He glanced around quickly to see if anyone was staring at him. Nobody was. The other boys were busy changing for football and paid little attention as he went to his peg and began, still cautiously, to undress. By the time he was pulling on his stripy socks, Slugger had seen every last part of himself and was confident of being 100 per cent non-baboon. Determined to regain some cool, he looked around for someone to bully. Four pegs away, and trying not to be noticed, was Ned Trotter.

Slugger pitched in. 'Oh, no – Nerdy Ned's

going to play football. Are these your boots, Ned?' He picked a pair up from the bench.

'Y-yes,' stuttered Ned.

Slugger tutted. 'There's a bit of mud on this one, Ned. You can't play football with dirty boots.'

'S-sorry,' stammered Ned. Oli rolled his eyes. There was no hope for the boy.

'Tell you what, Ned,' Slugger went on. 'I'll wash it for you.' And he turned towards the loos.

'Do something, Ned,' urged Oli, 'Go on.'

Ned took a deep breath, shot a glance at Oli for reassurance, and squeaked, 'Leave my boots alone!'

Slugger ignored him. 'Just a drop of water and they'll be as good as new,' he called over his shoulder.

A jostle of boys clustered round the cubicle door as Slugger held the hijacked footwear over the loo. Ned could only watch with a plummeting heart as his boot was dropped.

It bounced off the cling film and clattered onto the floor. The crowd roared. Slugger, purple with fury at being caught out by his own booby-

trap, spun round to face Ned.

'This is all your fault,' he growled and he began lumbering forwards, like an angry bear after a quivering chipmunk.

'Eek!' squealed Ned and scurried away towards the changing-room doors. But Slugger was right behind him and Ned was seconds from being torn to bits, like his magazine, when Slugger screeched to a halt.

He had seen the blue-faced baboon again. This was

no trick of the light; this was no figment of his imagination. This was definitely a blue-faced baboon, running past the row of mirrors exactly as he was running past them.

'No!' yelled Slugger in anguish. Burying his face in his hands, he shot back into the nearest cubicle and slammed the lock. Once more, laughter and wisecracks filled the air. Slugger cowered in miserable silence until the last of the boys had clattered out of the changing rooms. Then he unlocked his door, peeked out and crept back to the mirrors.

He squinted fearfully into the first one. The baboon squinted back. He tried the next one. There it was again. Blue cheeks and a bright red nose, lots of fur. Slugger raised an arm. The baboon raised an arm. Slugger stuck his tongue out. The baboon stuck his tongue back. Slugger opened his mouth wide and saw huge canine teeth.

He sank to the floor with a groan. He had seen pictures of that baboon with the blue and red face. It had a blue bum, too. A blue bum! Filled with foreboding, Slugger climbed onto one of the basins and perched unsteadily while he pulled down his football shorts and underpants, twisting to see his bottom in the mirror. Sure enough – sticking out above the shorts in the mirror was a patch of blue in a thick mass of brown fur.

Suddenly the doors opened and in came Oli.

Slugger stumbled off the basin and collapsed onto the floor, trying to pull his shorts up over his bottom. Oli stopped and stared down at the strange sight of Slugger, writhing about on the tiles like a huge maggot. Then he walked across to his peg, picked up his goalie gloves, and walked out, shaking his head.

Slugger staggered to his own peg and changed back into his school clothes as fast as his trembling hands would allow. With no thought beyond getting away from the school and everyone in it, he legged it from the changing room and down the corridor towards the main entrance. He would wait outside in the car park until his mum came to collect him.

The door to freedom was almost within his

grasp when a voice behind him called out,
'Melvyn! Stop!'

His hopes crashed and burned. Slugger turned
round to see Miss Green coming towards him.

'Why aren't you playing football?' she asked.

'I don't feel well,' mumbled Slugger. 'I was
going to wait outside for my mum.'

'Until half past four? Tut, tut – we can't have
that, Melvyn. You might be abducted by aliens
again. You'll have to come and wait in the art
room. You could even join in. We're doing self-
portraits.'

Slugger followed Miss Green into the art room
where fourteen girls were sitting in a row with
pads of paper, concentrating on reproducing
themselves beautifully in pastels. Propped against

the wall in front of them was an enormous mirror.

'Argh!' shouted Slugger leaping sideways so that he was out of range.

'Don't be shy, Melvyn,' said Miss Green crisply as she pulled another chair to the end of the row. 'Leonardo da Vinci painted himself several times and he was no beauty either.'

'I – I'm not feeling well,' mumbled Slugger and he sank to the floor. 'I'll just wait here.' While fourteen little artists tittered, Slugger closed his eyes and wished the whole wide world would go away.

Like many goalies, Oli had never actually volunteered for the job. His coach had simply scanned the team one day and picked the boy least likely to say, 'But, sir!' On his first stint between the posts Oli had hopped about anxiously and let in six goals, including two of his own. But he had learnt a lot since then.

The team trained hard for an hour and Oli had no time to reflect on Slugger's bizarre acrobatics on the changing-room basin. Later, however, while he and Skipjack were waiting by the school gates for Tara, they spotted a familiar figure hurrying across the car park.

'Look, there goes Slugger,' remarked Skipjack. 'Hey, Slugger,' he called, 'have you thought about a head transplant?'

But Slugger kept his head down and dived into a waiting car.

'He didn't swear at me or shake his fist,' commented Skipjack, surprised. 'He didn't even threaten to jump up and down on my head. He can't be well.'

'He's not,' said Oli. 'I haven't had a chance to tell you what he was doing in the changing room when I went back for my gloves. This will blow you over. He was standing on the basin with his shorts round his ankles, looking at his bum in the mirror!'

'You mean – doing a moony?' giggled Skipjack.

'A full moony. When I went in he jumped off the basin and sort of crouched underneath, like he was hiding from me. It was really weird.'

'I ran into Mr Surd being weird, too,' Skipjack

remembered.

'Yeah, but Mr Surd is always weird,' Oli pointed out. 'It would be weird to run into Mr Surd not being weird.'

'I know, but this was extra weird, even by his standards. I crashed into him in the corridor and instead of yelling at me and giving me a detention, he just kind of crouched there, hiding his face behind some bits of paper.'

'Perhaps there is a Weird Disease going around,' said Oli. 'I wish Tara would hurry up.'

'I saw her on my way here telling Katie Adams her fortune. I hope I don't feature in it.'

'I thought you liked Katie Adams?'

'I like the sweets she leaves in my desk.'

Tara had turned her Fortune Telling Bones into a useful source of cash by offering readings to friends and fellow pupils. She appeared at last, grinning with satisfaction.

'I've just earned 50p by telling Katie Adams that she is really the long-lost daughter of King Olaf of Fairytania and that when she grows up she'll marry a prince,' she announced. 'I'm getting really good at thinking these things up.

Soon I'll have enough money for my ticket to Timbuktu.'

'Don't you ever feel guilty about not telling the truth?' asked Oli.

Tara looked blank. 'Of course not. No one wants to know the truth.'

'I suppose when the prince turns up it'll be the end of my sweets,' remarked Skipjack gloomily. 'Hey, Tara, have you seen anyone being weird today? We think there is a weird disease going round the school.'

'Only Slugger,' said Tara. 'Miss Green made him come and wait in the art room and he took one look at us all sitting in front of the mirror and collapsed on the floor by the wall and that's where he stayed until home time. Is that weird enough?'

'It sure is. Slugger again,' said Oli thoughtfully.

'And mirrors again,' added Skipjack.

'He's a vampire,' announced Tara. 'Vampires have to avoid mirrors coz they have no reflection.'

'But why did he want to look at his bum?' asked Oli.

'He's just a very rude vampire.' Tara, as usual, had an answer for everything.

'Mr Surd definitely looks like a vampire,' said Skipjack.

'You should take a mirror to school,' Tara told them. 'Then you can look at Slugger and Mr Surd in it and if you don't see their reflections you'll know they're vampires.'

'Good idea,' agreed Oli. 'Becky's got lots of little mirrors. I'll borrow one of hers.'

'And I'll make a wooden stake with my penknife,' said Skipjack happily. 'Whoever thought Mr Surd and Slugger would give us this much fun?'

5
Scary Hairy Slugger

At 7.27 precisely on Wednesday morning, the
alarm clock beside Mr Vernon Surd's narrow
iron bed began to ring. Mr Surd reached out a
long, bony arm and pressed the snooze button.
He did not want to get up.

At about 7.40 a.m., having once again alarmed
the birds and Mrs Higginbottom, Slugger's
mother marched in to her son's room to rip away
the bedclothes and was astonished to find his bed
empty. She went to the bathroom and banged on
the locked door.

'Melvyn? Is that you in there?'

'Yeah, Mum.' Slugger was staring at his blue-
faced, hairy self in the mirror. He was deeply
depressed. He had hoped that a new dawn
might bring an end to the baboon nightmare.

On returning home from school the previous afternoon, he had tried every single mirror in the house and he had looked like a baboon in all of them. The only consolation was that other people didn't seem to notice; he just had to make sure that nobody saw his reflection.

Slugger left the bathroom a moment later. He never bothered much about washing and seeing only a baboon in the mirror gave him the perfect excuse not to bother at all. Anyway, he had no intention of going into school today. Before pushing open the kitchen door, Slugger arranged his face to look as sick as possible.

'Mum,' he mumbled, 'I don't feel very well. Can I stay at home today?'

His mother placed a rough hand briefly to his forehead. 'There's nothing wrong with you, Melvyn. I won't have you skiving again. Hurry up and eat your breakfast.'

At 7.45 a.m., Oli had his ear cocked for the sound of his sister Becky going downstairs. Ah-ha – that was her. She should be reaching the kitchen about . . . now. Oli flung open his door and sprinted along the corridor to Becky's room. There he stopped in dismay. What a mess! How was he supposed to find a tiny mirror in a jumble like this?

'Stand aside,' commanded Tara from behind him. 'I know where she keeps them.' She went straight to a drawer, pulled it open and picked out a purple thing covered with pearly pink flowers. 'This is what you want,' she said, tossing it to him. 'It's called a compact.'

'Hasn't she got a smaller one?' asked Oli, holding the offending item by one corner as if it would contaminate him with girliness.

'Don't be so pathetic,' said his sister. 'Do you want to find out whether Slugger and Mr Surd are vampires or don't you?'

'All right, all right. How do I open it?'

Tara showed him the clasp and Oli opened the compact. 'It's got make-up inside!' he wailed.

'It's called powder,' Tara told him.

'Yuk. I'll have to be really careful about using this thing. I don't want anyone to think I'm putting make-up on. Yuk.'

Vernon Surd finally dragged himself out of bed and hobbled along the bare floorboards to his chilly bathroom, where he gazed miserably in the mirror. A pair of beady black eyes glared back at him out of a scabby, bald red face with a long, hooked grey beak. Sagging folds of skin drooped from his throat, which stuck out from a collar of greasy black feathers. He sighed.

Oli showed Becky's mirror to Skipjack before

they left for school. Skipjack was horrified. 'You can't take that to school – what if someone sees you?'

'I'll just have to risk that,' Oli told him heroically. 'It takes courage to be a vampire hunter.'

'Well, that rules me out,' said Skipjack.

Just then Oli caught wind of a mysterious odour. He leaned closer to his friend and sniffed. 'What did you have for breakfast, Skip?'

'It's not my breakfast you're smelling – it's this.' From his bulging pockets Skipjack produced several fat bulbs of garlic. 'They always use it in films to ward off vampires,' he explained. 'I thought I wouldn't take any chances.'

Oli held his nose. 'Don't worry, Skip – you'll ward off *everybody*.'

'Good morning, Mr Surd,' called Albert Grimble from the wheel of his shiny new Number 11. 'Did you remember your camera today?'

Mr Surd shuffled aboard, frowning. 'No. I had other things on my mind.'

Mr Grimble took a close look at his passenger.

'You're not looking yourself today if I might say so,' he remarked.

Mr Surd put a hand up to feel the plasters that were stuck all over his stubbly face, evidence of a disastrous attempt at shaving when all he could see in the mirror was a vulture. 'I'm not exactly feeling myself,' he muttered.

'You must come by the bus station this week, Mr Surd,' continued Albert Grimble in a rare chatty mood. 'We've got a new Number 22 on loan from the Bilchester and District Monarch line. She's a beauty."

'I'm sure she is,' said Mr Surd and escaped to the back of the bus as fast as he could limp.

Keen though Oli was to discover whether Slugger was now Count Slugger, producing a pearly pink powder compact at school was no easy task. And Slugger himself was making it even less easy by skulking alone in corners and darting away whenever Oli tried to edge closer. Oli finally spotted his chance in Science, when the class was divided into groups and allowed to move around the room. Choosing a moment when everyone was busy looking at pictures of micro-organisms, Oli positioned himself with his back to his suspect and took the compact from his pocket. Bracing himself for the shock of seeing no reflection of Slugger in the mirror, he opened the compact for a peep.

Right behind him was an enormous baboon! 'ARGH!' yelled Oli, leaping away and knocking over several chairs.

Miss Green looked up from the other side of the room. 'Whatever is the matter, Oli?'

Oli glanced around fearfully, but the baboon had completely disappeared. He stuffed the compact back in his pocket. 'Nothing, Miss Green. Sorry.'

The rest of the class were giggling, except Slugger who was eyeing Oli with deep suspicion. Unfortunately, Miss Green kept him under surveillance as well, so for a while it was impossible to use the mirror again.

Skipjack kept sidling up, like a very keen trainee in the Penguin Secret Service, to nudge him and murmur, 'Well?' out of the corner of his mouth.

'Not sure yet,' replied Oli. 'I need another look.'

Finally, Katie Adams saw a picture of a tapeworm and helpfully fainted. This occupied all the girls and Miss Green for long enough for Oli to sneak another peek in the mirror.

There was the baboon again! This time Oli

managed not to yell or knock any chairs over, even though it was a very ugly beast. Strangely, it appeared to be sitting in Slugger's seat, flicking balls of paper off the end of a ruler. Oli peeped cautiously over his shoulder. There was Slugger, sitting in Slugger's seat, flicking balls of paper off the end of a ruler.

The penny was beginning to drop.

Oli looked in the mirror again. Baboon. Oli looked over his shoulder again. Slugger. Oli closed the compact, and grinned.

'So let me get this straight,' said Skipjack in break. 'When you looked in the mirror, Slugger was a baboon?'

'That's right,' chuckled Oli. 'The really ugly kind with the blue face and the red nose.'

'So that's what Slugger sees every time he looks at himself?'

'It must be. Which is why I caught him looking at his bum in the changing room. He wanted to see if it was blue!'

Both boys collapsed. 'This is immense!' cried Skipjack when he could speak again. He wiped the tears from his eyes. 'Look – here he comes. Hi, Slugger. You look very serious today. Why aren't you monkeying around like you usually do?'

Slugger clenched his fists. 'Shut up, Haynes,' he muttered without looking up.

'OK, Slugger. By the way – what did you have for breakfast today, Slugger – bananas?'

Oli snorted. Slugger made a strange sound like a blocked drain and marched away.

Skipjack asked, 'Do you think Mr Surd is a baboon as well?'

'Well, we've got maths next,' replied Oli, 'so we'll soon find out.'

But Vernon Surd had taken one look at the school from the bus stop and climbed straight back on the Number 11.

'You're right, Mr Grimble,' he had muttered as he hobbled back to his seat. 'I don't feel well at all. I think I shall go back home to bed.'

So it was Miss Green who arrived to take the maths lesson instead.

'I understand you were doing fractions,' she said, 'and some of you were finding them a bit tricky. Fractions aren't tricky, they're dead simple. Like with all maths, you just have to keep a cool head. Everyone got their cool heads on? Let's go.'

The next forty minutes brought a revelation during which Oli discovered that he could not only do fractions after all, but he quite enjoyed doing them. By the end of the lesson he realised with relief that his problem was not with maths at all, just with Mr Surd.

At lunchtime Tara came looking for him. 'Well, are they vampires?' she demanded.

'No, baboons,' Oli told her.

'Baboons?'

'Baboons. At least, Slugger's a baboon. We haven't been able to test Mr Surd yet, cos he's not in.'

'Uh-oh,' said Tara, shaking her head.

'Why "uh-oh"?' enquired Oli.

'Because, what are you going to do about it?' asked Tara.

'What do you mean, "What am I going to do about it"? It's nothing to do with me.'

'Of course it is. It must have been your mirror

that turned them into baboons. It can't be a coincidence that on Monday you get a magic mirror and on Tuesday the reflections of the two people you most hate turn into baboons. You must have put some sort of curse on them. Boy, will they be angry when they find out.'

'She has a point,' put in Skipjack.

'It's ridiculous!' insisted Oli. 'That mirror is just a souvenir, like your death mask and Tara's bones. It can't possibly have magic powers —' Oli paused, '— can it?' He remembered how he had sat in bed the previous morning, glaring into the mirror and wishing with all his might that Slugger and Mr Surd would disappear. He gulped.

'Let's have a good look at it after school,' suggested Skipjack. 'We might find a clue.'

A Smashing Time

In Oli and Tara's garden was a tree house, with a proper roof and windows and a trapdoor in the floor, from which a rope ladder hung down to the ground. This was the stronghold where secrets were discussed, plans hatched and refuge taken from angry mums, bus drivers and other grown-ups on the warpath.

The tree house was also home to Tara's collection of pets. Tara's pets were the sort that could be picked up for free in the garden and several shelves were occupied by snails, crickets and woodlice sliding, hopping and scuttling about in various cages. There was also a hospital wing, where dehydrated frogs and three-legged spiders were nursed until the inevitable happened. Then their remains were donated to science, which meant that they were chopped up and examined through a magnifying glass. The more interesting samples were preserved in malt vinegar, with the result that several more shelves were filled with strange specimens floating in jars of dark liquid.

It was to the tree house that Oli, Skipjack and Tara came after school, for a secret inspection of the mirror. The danger of disturbance was

low: Mrs Biggles was still at work and Oli's older sister Becky, who was supposed to be in charge, believed in ruling from a distance.

'It smells like a chip shop in here,' commented Skipjack as he pulled himself up through the trap door.

'It's the vinegar,' explained Oli. 'Tara's been doing more pickling.'

'It's making me hungry,' sighed Skipjack and opened both windows wide.

Oli examined the mirror thoroughly, pressing, turning and pulling all the carved chameleons in its frame that looked as if they might press, turn or pull.

'Does it have an on/off switch?' asked Skipjack.

'No, Skip. There's nothing to tell us how the spell started or how to stop it.'

'It's not a spell so much as a curse,' said Tara. 'The chameleons have given Slugger and Mr Surd the Evil Eye.'

'Perhaps Sid can help,' suggested Skipjack. 'She gave you the mirror, so she might know its secrets. Isn't she due back today?'

'Of course!' exclaimed Oli. 'Let's go and give her a ring.'

'She might say, "Come round for pizza",' said Skipjack hopefully.

So the three children shinned down the rope ladder and ran into the house. Skipjack and Tara gathered round the phone while Oli dialled the number for Mrs Happy's Pizzas and waited for a connection. At last he gave them a thumbs-up.

'Sid? Is that you? Phew! It's Oli . . . Fine thanks, Sid . . . Yeah, so is Tara . . . Yeah, he's fine, too, apart from missing your triple-pepperoni pizzas . . . In trouble? What makes you say that? . . . Not always, Sid – just occasionally. Well, as a matter of fact . . . Can we? Thanks, Sid. See you later.'

He put the phone down.

'Well?' demanded Skipjack.

'She says come round for pizza.'

'Yippee!'

'I can't come,' grumbled Tara. 'I've got to do my homework before Mum takes me to swimming practice.'

'Will you tell her where we've gone?' asked

Oli. 'I'll go and get the mirror.'

'I'll just wait for you here,' said Skipjack, who had spotted the tin which he knew was the official residence of the Biggles' chocolate chip cookies.

The Oli who approached the tree house did so with a much lighter step than the Oli who had approached it last. He even whistled. Sid, his own personal knight in shining armour, was back and all his troubles would be solved.

Little did he realise that his troubles were about to get a good deal worse. Halfway up the ladder, he heard a noise from inside the tree house. He paused for a moment before deciding it was probably one of Tara's animals, rustling in its leaves. He continued to the top and stuck his head up through the open trapdoor.

Inside the tree house, standing by the table on which lay the mirror, was Slugger Stubbins.

'Slugger!' gasped Oli.

The invader spun round. He recognised the head. He scowled at it. 'Explain this, Biggles!' he demanded, jabbing a finger at the mirror.

'Ah. Er, it's a mirror.'

'I know it's a mirror, you blockhead!' shouted Slugger. 'And I know you used it to put a curse on me. Now I want you to take the curse off. Take it off, Biggles, or you'll be very, very sorry.'

Slugger took a step towards the trapdoor and Oli realised two things very quickly. First, that Slugger had feet the size of aircraft carriers and second, that his own head, being level with those feet, was in a dangerous place. He climbed up into the tree house. Then putting on the Innocent Puppy face he had learnt from Skipjack, he asked, 'What makes you think I've got anything to do with this curse?'

'Because I heard you say so ten minutes ago,' retorted Slugger. 'I got suspicious after Haynes cracked all those jokes about monkeys and bananas, so I followed you back after school and listened in the bushes.'

Oli shook his head sadly. 'Tut, tut, Slugger. People who eavesdrop –'

Slugger leapt forwards, grabbed Oli by the collar and pinned him against a wall. 'What have you done to me?' he demanded.

'I don't know,' gasped Oli.

'Well, whatever it is, undo it now!'

'But I don't know how to undo what I didn't know I did!' cried Oli, 'Especially if I don't know how I did it.'

'You don't know very much, do you?' Slugger dropped Oli and returned to the table, where he picked up the mirror. 'Well, I know one thing: this mirror is the cause of my trouble. So, no more mirror, no more trouble.'

'Don't!' shouted Oli, but Slugger threw the mirror down on the floor. There was a blinding flash. Slugger turned into a baboon.

The baboon stopped dead. He held up his hairy monkey hands and looked down at his hairy monkey body. He picked up his hairy monkey tail. Oli, momentarily frozen with shock, recovered his wits fast enough to make his escape. Scrambling down the first few rungs of the rope ladder, he pulled the trapdoor down and shot home the bolt that kept it in place. Then with trembling fingers he slithered down the rest of the ladder, while furious thumps shuddered the tree house floor above him.

He ran into Skipjack just coming out of the

back door.

'What's that noise?' mumbled Skipjack through a mouthful of cookie.

'It's Slugger,' panted Oli. 'I found him in the tree house. He smashed the mirror and now he's turned into a *real* baboon!'

'Awesome!'

'What are we going to do about it?'

'Sell tickets to see him?'

'Be serious, Skip! This is an emergency!'

They looked up at the tree house. A furry brown streak shot past the window. Then it shot back again. Then there was a crash. Oli winced.

'There go Tara's samples,' remarked Skipjack as the air was filled with vinegar fumes. 'And look – there's Slugger!'

Sure enough, an angry blue face had appeared at the small window to glare at them. Skipjack gave it a little wave.

'I wish I had my camera,' he sighed.

'I wish you had an idea how to get me out of this,' said his friend.

'OK, Oli. But let's go inside. I can't concentrate out here cos I keep thinking of chips.'

When they were back in the kitchen Skipjack said, 'First we should go and check on Mr Surd.'

'Mr Surd!' cried Oli. 'I blogging well hope he hasn't turned into a baboon as well!'

'We'll soon find out,' said Skipjack. 'Where does he live?'

'Where does who live?' asked Tara, who had come down for a cookie.

Oli told her what had happened. Tara was fascinated to learn of Slugger's transformation.

'Has he got a blue bottom?' was her first question.

'Funnily enough, I didn't hang around to find out,' said Oli. 'Er, Tara, I think he might have smashed one or two of your samples.'

His little sister frowned. Finally she said, 'I *almost* don't mind, as you've been brilliant enough to turn Slugger into a baboon.'

Oli looked relieved. 'I'll go and look up Mr Surd's address in the phone book. There can't be too many Surds in this town, although even one is too many.'

He dashed into the hall and dashed out again seconds later, waving a torn sheet from the telephone directory.

'Leek Street,' he said. 'It's behind the bus station. Number 2.' He turned to Tara. 'Can you phone Sid for us, to say we'll be a bit late? And will you try to keep Mum busy, so she doesn't notice Slugger crashing around in the tree house?'

'OK. If she hears him I'll pretend I'm keeping a stray cat up there,' said Tara, opening the cookie tin. 'A really wild one. Hey, where are all the cookies? Skipjack!'

But the boys had gone, hurrying on their bikes towards Mr Surd's house and wondering what they would find.

Tara went outside to laugh at Slugger for a while. Then she had an idea and she went up to her room to write a letter to the local zoo.

Leek Street was a long row of tall, thin, semi-detached houses. The boys approached Number 2 with caution, keeping a sharp look-out for baboons.

They leaned their bikes against the garden wall and Oli pressed the front door bell. They waited. And waited. Oli looked at the bare and weedy front garden and the peeling paint around the dusty windows. Skipjack peered in at a small, empty sitting room.

'At least he's not crashing around like Slugger was,' he remarked. 'Perhaps he really is just ill.'

'Let's go and peek through a back window,' said Oli and he led the way up the side path to the rear garden. They positioned themselves beneath the nearest window and on Oli's count of three they raised their heads cautiously and peeped inside.

Perched on the back of a kitchen chair was a vulture.

The big, black bird sat, hunched and motionless, frowning into the gloom of Mr Surd's kitchen. On the table stood an unfinished plate of sardines on toast and a glass of water.

The boys stared for a moment and then lowered themselves beneath the window again.

'A vulture is much better,' said Skipjack approvingly. 'Mr Surd isn't at all like a baboon.'

But Oli was in shock. How many detentions would he get for turning his maths teacher into a vulture?

'Let's get away from here,' he muttered. 'We must make a plan.'

Once they had put some distance between themselves and the new, feathered Mr Surd, Oli began to calm down.

'At least there was no sign of a Mrs Surd or

any other Surds,' he said, 'so he might not be discovered for a while. The first thing we must do is to move Slugger from the tree house before he's discovered. Then we'll go and see Sid and find out how to de-curse them. That way Slugger will be nice and far away when he turns back into Slugger and he won't be able to thump me.'

'But where shall we move him to?' asked Skipjack.

'It'll have to be Mr Surd's house,' replied Oli. 'No one will see him there. Except Mr Surd, of course.'

'But that's halfway across town! How are we going to get him there? How are we even going to catch him without being shredded alive?'

'Wild animals are always caught with food,' said Oli. 'What's Slugger's favourite food?'

'Chips,' said Skipjack without hesitation.

'Right. We'll lure him out of the tree house with chips and while he's busy eating we'll creep up behind him and throw my camouflage net over him.' Oli began to cheer up; he liked this sort of plan. 'Then we'll put him in a bag. There's a great big canvas bag at home that the tent packs into. It's really strong, with drawstrings.'

'Oh, please can we carry the bag like they do in jungle movies,' begged Skipjack, 'tied to the middle of a long pole with one of us holding each end?'

So they stopped at the chip shop and bought two extra large portions with ketchup.

'I'll put these in the bike shed until Mum's out of the way,' said Oli.

'I could stay and guard them,' offered Skipjack, licking his lips.

'From what, Skip?'

'Er . . . squirrels?'

But Oli, who knew his friend well, pointed out that he could just shut the shed door and that, unless there was a sudden attack of Giant Shed-Door-Opening Squirrels, the chips should be quite safe. With the baboon bait stashed away, they went into the house.

'We're home, Mum!' called Oli. 'Can Skipjack stay so we can do our homework together?'

'Hi, boys. As long as he rings his mum to tell her. Tara, I think you'll have to let that cat go tonight. None of us will get any sleep with all that yowling.'

She'll quieten down, Mum,' replied Tara with a wink at the boys. 'She's just frightened.'

'Hm. We'll decide when we get back from swimming. Come on.'

As soon as Mum and Tara had gone, the boys sprang into action. While Oli found the net, the tent bag and a long pole, Skipjack collected the chips and managed to eat only six before placing them on the grass directly below the tree house. Then the brave baboon-hunters met behind the tree for a final rundown.

'One of us has to hide here with the net,' said Oli in a low voice, 'and the other one has to climb up the ladder, open the trap door and climb down again really quickly before Slugger catches up with him.'

Skipjack nodded. 'I'll do the net part,' he said.

'I thought you would. I'll do the suicidal part. Here goes.'

'Hold on,' said Skipjack, feeling a twinge of guilt. 'This will make it less suicidal: Ta-da!' From his back pocket he produced his trusty

catapult. 'If we aim some chips through the window, Slugger might start eating them and not notice you opening the trapdoor. Then you'll have more time to escape.'

'Skip, your brain is the eighth wonder of the world.'

Years of practice had formed Skipjack into a hot-shot catapulter and soon chips were flying through the air and into the tree house. He continued firing until Oli reached the trap door and then he put away his catapult, ate a couple more chips and took up his post behind the tree. Here he tried to arrange the net in such a way that he would be able to throw it over Slugger without, he hoped, entangling himself as well.

At the top of the ladder Oli paused to listen. He could hear munching noises; Slugger was enjoying his chips. It's now or never, thought Oli and he shot back the bolt and flung open the trapdoor. A livid screech came from inside as Oli slithered back down the rope ladder and legged it round the corner of the house.

He stood there for a moment with his back to the wall, panting hard. Then he peeped carefully round to the tree house.

Slugger was peering down through the trapdoor. As Oli watched, he swung out and began to climb down the ladder. Oli could see Skipjack pop his head round the tree and pop it back again. At the foot of the ladder, Slugger stopped. Would he go for the chips?

'Come on, come on,' muttered Oli.

Slugger looked round, sniffing. It occurred to Oli that they had no Plan B; if Slugger simply ran away, there was nothing they could do. Oli tried not to think how much trouble he would be in then.

But Slugger had seen the chips. He approached them slowly on all fours, sat down next to them and began to eat.

Skipjack's head appeared once more round the tree and his eyebrows shot up at the sight of the feasting baboon. A look of intense concentration spread to the tip of his tongue as he crept forwards with the net. At the last minute Slugger looked round but he was too late: Skipjack flung the net over him and he was trapped.

Slugger screeched and struggled but the more he fought to free himself the more entangled he became. Then Oli arrived with the canvas bag and the team managed to bundle their prisoner into it, without being bitten. They quickly drew the strings as tightly as possible and Oli tied several firm knots.

'Phew! That's that. Let's try the pole.'

'Listen to his screeches,' giggled Skipjack. 'Those must be really naughty baboon swear words.'

They threaded the pole through the loops of rope, took an end each and heaved. But Slugger

was an extra big baboon and the boys could not lift him more than an inch or two off the ground.

'We'll never be able to carry him all the way to Mr Surd's house,' panted Skipjack as they dropped him back on the grass. 'He's just too fat. What now?'

What indeed. What if Slugger was still sitting in his bag on the grass when Mum came back? Oli was just teetering on the brink of panic when inspiration held out a hand.

'My go-kart!' he cried and he ran back to the shed.

Skipjack collapsed onto the grass near – but not too near – the bundle of angry baboon. His eye fell on the unfinished chips and he was just wondering whether Slugger had infested them with fleas when Oli returned.

The go-kart was large and sturdy with a wooden seat onto which they managed to haul their loudly protesting captive. They strapped him on with elastic bungees and then they set off, with Oli pulling from the front and Skipjack pushing from the back.

'He's quietened down a bit,' Skipjack

observed. 'Perhaps he's enjoying the ride.'

'More likely he's just catching his breath before his next escape attempt,' said Oli. 'We're getting close to the bus station. Look out for Mr Grimble. He would be very suspicious if he spotted us.'

But Skipjack was defiant. 'Ha! Let him be suspicious! He can't do a thing from inside his bus. If I see him suspishing I shall look really guilty on purpose and make him suspish all the more.'

At that moment they rounded a corner, and who should they see bearing down on them but Mr Grimble himself. On foot.

'Mr Grimble!' exclaimed Oli.

'Where's your bus?' demanded Skipjack.

'I've just come off duty, not that it's any of your business,' muttered Albert Grimble. He took one look at the bundle on the go-kart and was instantly very suspicious.

'What have you got in that bag?' he demanded.

'Rugby balls,' said Skipjack. 'We're taking them to the club.'

'Ooh-ooh!' screeched Slugger, who had

apparently decided to attract Mr Grimble's attention in the hope of being rescued.

'Ooh-ooh-!' sang Skipjack at once, very loudly. 'I love you, please be true, baby!'

Mr Grimble frowned. 'That's not rugby balls. You've got someone in there. Who is it?'

'I can see you're much too clever for us, Mr Grimble,' said Oli with what he hoped was a disarming smile. 'As a matter of fact, it's my sister Tara. We're playing a game, you see. We pull her round the town in a bag and she has to say where she thinks she is. Say hello to Mr Grimble, Tara!'

'Eeh-eeh!' screeched Slugger, wriggling as much as the bungees would allow.

'And she has to speak in monkey language, too,' added Skipjack hurriedly. '"Eeh-eeh" means "Hello, Mr Grimble". Well, we must go. Come along, Tara.'

'Oooh!' screeched Slugger as the boys hurried away.

'I hope he's not going to follow us,' said Skipjack, glancing over his shoulder. But luckily Mr Grimble was even more tired and hungry than he was suspicious, and decided to go home for a nice cup of tea and some onion pie.

Soon Slugger was being pushed and pulled up the path of No. 2 Leek Street. When they reached the back garden, Oli glanced through the kitchen window. Mr Surd was still perched on the back of the chair but the sardines on toast had vanished. Oli tried the back door, hoping it was not locked. It opened, but with a squeak which made Mr Surd look round. When he saw Oli, the maths teacher glared at him in just the same way he always did in lessons. Then he unfurled his enormous wings. Oli could not believe the size of those wings – they stretched from one side of the kitchen to the other. Then Mr Surd gave a flap, keeping his beady eyes fixed on Oli, who looked at the sharp beak and the long talons and closed the door hastily.

He turned to Skipjack. 'It isn't going to be easy to get Slugger in there. If the door is open for too long Mr Surd might fly out. He might even attack us. He is looking a teensy bit cross.'

'They go for the eyeballs first,' said Skipjack helpfully.

Oli looked around the barren back yard for something that could be used as a Vulture Defence Weapon. He spotted a plastic garden chair. Hardly an anti-aircraft missile, but better

than nothing.

'We can use that to block the doorway,' he said. Skipjack fetched the chair doubtfully.

They heaved Slugger off the go-kart and dragged him, kicking and cursing, to the door.

'I'll just loosen the strings on his bag,' said Oli. 'He'll find his own way out. Ready? Here goes.' He threw the door open and gave the bag a mighty push. It may have been Skipjack's brave waving of the plastic chair that discouraged Mr Surd from attempting attack or escape, or he may have been distracted by the arrival of a large and squirming canvas bag in his kitchen. Either way he missed his chance and as Slugger, with one last shove, went skidding across the lino, Oli slammed the door shut with relief.

'Phew – that's that. Let's go to Sid's place.'

8
Zomu's Spell

Sid was behind the counter slicing up a pizza when the boys walked in. 'Hiya, Oli! Hiya, Skip!' she called, beaming, when she saw them. 'You're just in time to try my new pizza – it's Africa-flavoured!' She slid two fat wedges onto plates and pushed them towards the boys. 'Sit down, guys. Did you miss me?'

'We missed your pizza a lot,' Skipjack told her. 'No one makes pizza like you, Sid.'

'And we missed your help,' said Oli.

'Go on then,' chuckled Sid. 'Tell me about the latest trouble.'

'It's that mirror, Sid,' began Oli. 'It's had a strange effect on Slugger.'

'That sounds good. It hasn't turned him into a human being, by any chance?'

'That would be more than strange,' remarked

Skipjack. 'That would be a miracle. This new pizza's great, Sid. What's in it?'

'Well, it's meant to be bush rat . . .'

Skipjack's jaws froze.

'But I had to use chicken.'

Skipjack started chewing again.

'And peanut butter, and a sprinkling of secret herbs and spices. Tell me more about Slugger.'

'He's a baboon.'

'I know that. I mean, what's the mirror done?'

'Just that, Sid. It's turned him into a baboon.'

'The sort with a blue and red face and a blue bum,' added Skipjack.

Sid's face started to twitch and then she threw back her head and roared. 'That's smashing,' she said at last, wiping her eyes. 'What a shame you can't leave him like that.'

'I've also turned our maths teacher, Mr Surd, into a vulture.'

'That's a bit more serious. How?'

'No idea,' said Oli. 'Mr Surd and Slugger were both being massively mean – Slugger thumped me in the stomach so hard I couldn't breathe for hours and Mr Surd told everyone I was the stupidest boy in the class, so I was really angry with them both. Then they started acting very weird and we discovered that their reflections had changed and then Slugger worked out that we had something to do with it and followed us to the tree house. He found your mirror and smashed it, and that's when he really did turn into a baboon.'

'Do you think,' wondered Skipjack, 'that if he looked in the mirror now he would see a baboon, or Slugger?'

'Where are they?' asked Sid.

'They're both at Mr Surd's house. The problem is that I've got no idea how they turned into animals in the first place, so I've got no idea how to turn them back again.'

'I don't suppose that mirror came with any instructions, did it?' asked Skipjack. 'Or a nice three-year guarantee against magic accidents?'

'I'm afraid not.'

'What about the medicine man you got it from?' asked Oli. 'Did he say anything that might help?'

Sid shook her head. 'All Zomu said was that the mirror had magic powers.'

'Well he was right about that,' sighed Oli. 'What are we going to do, Sid? I mean, I can't go all the way to Africa to find your medicine man and ask him how to fix this.'

'There are other ways,' said Sid mysteriously, 'of contacting medicine men.'

Oli's eyes widened. 'You mean mind-reading

and witchcraft and black magic?'

'Nope. I mean telephones. Zomu loves  gadgets. He's never without his mobile. You stay here and finish your pizza; I'll go and ring him.'

A few minutes later she returned.

'Well?' demanded Oli.

'Well, it's very simple.'

'Oh, good,' said Oli.

'But it might not be easy.'

'Oh, bad,' said Skipjack.

'Is it a magic spell?' asked Oli.

'Kind of. You have to forgive them.'

'Forgive them?'

'Yes. You have to forgive Slugger for being such a bully and you have to forgive Mr Surd for being such a meanie. Then the curse will be lifted.'

'But, I don't want to

forgive them,' protested Oli. 'They aren't sorry, so why should I?'

'They don't have to be sorry,' Sid explained. 'This isn't about them, it's about you. As long as you stay angry with them, they will hang over you like big black clouds. Zomu says that Slugger might be a prisoner inside his baboon, and Mr Surd inside his vulture, but until you forgive them you are just as much of a prisoner inside your bad feelings. And I think he's right. Anyway,' she finished with a chuckle, 'nothing annoys your enemies as much as forgiving them.'

Oli bit off another hunk of pizza and chewed thoughtfully. He had to admit it made sense; he was fed up with hating Slugger and Mr Surd. He just wanted to forget about them both. Then he spotted a hitch. Mr Surd's kitchen, while not quite a lions' den, was not a place to linger in and he doubted if he would get much forgiving done before he was ripped apart. 'Can I forgive them through the window?' he asked.

'You can forgive them from here,' Sid told him. 'Zomu says you don't have to do it face to face – you just have to mean it.'

'What if Mr Surd calls me stupid again one day, or Slugger thumps me?'

'That might happen,' agreed Sid, 'but I don't think you'll mind Mr Surd calling you stupid any more, because you'll know it's his problem, not yours. As for Slugger, I think he'll be quite wary of you from now on.'

'OK,' said Oli. 'I forgive them.'

Sid beamed. 'Good for you. Now, I think you should race home before anyone worries about you. Ask if you can come and have some more Africa Pizza on Friday and I'll tell you the story of my close shave with a crocodile.'

The boys gasped. 'Where?' asked Skipjack.

'In my bath,' said Sid.

'It must have been a very big bath,' remarked Oli.

'Or a very small crocodile,' added Skipjack.

'Or a very tall story,' said Sid with a wink. 'Come back on Friday and you'll find out which.'

Mr Surd's kitchen, meanwhile, had in a flash stopped being a safari park. Slugger Stubbins, human again, would have had a good snigger at

the sight of Mr Surd
falling off his kitchen
chair if he hadn't
been so surprised to
find himself on top of
the cupboard.

'So it's you up
there, Stubbins,' said
Mr Surd, picking
himself up off the
floor. 'I hope you can
shed some light on
this outrage?'

'It was Oli Biggles,'
said Slugger, climbing
down to ground level.
'He cast a spell on us
using a magic mirror.'

'Don't be so
ridiculous,' said Mr
Surd. 'Spells – magic
– what nonsense. Talk
sense, boy.'

'It's true,' persisted

Slugger and he told Mr Surd the whole story.

Mr Surd frowned. It all sounded preposterous, yet there was no doubt that he had spent the last two hours as a vulture. Oh, the shame of it. A surge of anger rose up inside him as he imagined Oliver Biggles telling the whole school what he had done to the maths teacher. He was roused from these bitter thoughts by a cough from Slugger.

'I think I'll go now,' said the boy.

'No you won't,' Mr Surd told him. 'Not until we've made a plan for revenge.'

There was nothing Slugger loved more than making plans for revenge, apart from carrying them out, of course. He nodded eagerly. 'What shall we do, Mr Surd?'

'First, you must swear to keep all this a secret. If you go around saying Oliver Biggles turned you into a baboon you will be locked up for being stark staring mad and you will have no chance to get even. Is that understood?'

Slugger nodded vigorously. 'I won't tell,' he promised.

'Now then. We've got to get our hands on that

mirror. That's your job, Stubbins. Get it tonight and bring it to school in the morning.'

Slugger's face lit up. 'Are we going to put a spell on Biggles, Mr Surd?'

'We are, Stubbins, we are. We are going to turn him into a cockroach.' Mr Surd's eyes were gleaming. 'And then I shall stamp on him,' he said.

Unaware that the shadows of doom were stretching in his direction, Oli Biggles went to bed that night feeling peaceful and content. He had already decided that when he saw Mr Surd and Slugger the next day he would behave as if nothing had happened. If they chose to be friendlier in the light of their experience then he would be friendly, too; if not, so be it. He would never let them upset him so much again.

Oli had also decided not to tackle the tree house that evening. You cannot keep a big baboon in a small space for even a short time without ending up with a monster mess. He would need daylight, he would need mops and buckets and dustpans and brushes and gallons and gallons of disinfectant. He would also need Mum to be out, as the sight of her son with any of the above would ring loud alarm bells and lead to awkward questions being asked. He would find time at the weekend to clean up the tree house.

Later that night, Slugger Stubbins sneaked out of his bedroom, legged it to Oli's tree house and stole the mirror.

The Curse of the Uncursed

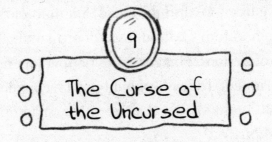

At 7.27 precisely on Thursday morning, the alarm clock beside Mr Vernon Surd's narrow iron bed began to beep. Mr Surd slammed it off and leapt out of bed. He washed, dressed and

shaved with grim purpose. Today he would pay Oli Biggles back.

At 7.30 a.m., more or less, Mrs Stubbins took a deep breath and yelled 'Melvyn!' up the stairs at top volume. There was the usual fluttering rumpus

in the tree tops and the usual dull thud of Mrs Higginbottom's bottom next door meeting her bedroom floor. Slugger's eyes popped open and he grinned. Today he would pay Oli Biggles back.

At 7.35 a.m., Oli Biggles was woken up by his sister marching in, pulling away his pillow and walloping him over the head with it.

'Ow!' cried Oli, cowering under the blows. 'What's that for?'

'This one is for Wiggly,' panted Tara with another wallop, 'and this one is for Scratchy, and this one is for Scamper. The other ones were for Mr and Mrs Woodlouse and all their babies.'

'What woodlice? What are you talking about?'

'My zoo,' Tara told him. 'Slugger ate it. My worm and my earwig and my spider. And a whole family of woodlice. It's mass murder. And he ate all my pickled specimens, too.'

Oli sat up. 'Even the toad?' he asked.

'Don't laugh!' She walloped him again. 'It's all smashed. And he's pooed everywhere as well.'

Suddenly it wasn't funny any more. Oli fell back on his remaining pillow with a groan. 'I'll clean it up on Saturday. And I'm sorry about Mr and Mrs Woodlouse, and Squiggly and Creepy and Grumpy. I'll find you some more.'

'You'd better. Well, what happened to Slugger?'

'We took him to Mr Surd's house and then Sid told us how to un-curse him.'

'Does that mean he's not a baboon any more?'

'I very much hope not.'

Tara sighed. 'Ah, well. Never mind.'

'You're looking much better today, Mr Surd,' said Albert Grimble approvingly. 'A remarkable recovery.'

'I feel much better, thank you,' replied his passenger.

'You still haven't been to the bus station to have a look at that Number 22,' Mr Grimble reminded him. 'She goes back to Bilchester on

Sunday and I'd hate you not to see her; she's a beautiful bus.'

'I shall make a point of coming by on Saturday,' replied Mr Surd. 'I wouldn't want to miss a rare chance like that.'

Mr Surd found Slugger Stubbins waiting in the Form 7 classroom for him as agreed, with a bulky package under his arm. The other children were outside in the playground and would not come in until the bell rang.

'I've got it!' hissed Slugger.

'Quick, take it out,' ordered Mr Surd.

He frowned when he saw that there was a long crack in the mirror, from when Slugger had smashed it in the tree house. 'I hope this doesn't reduce its effectiveness,' he murmured. 'But that is a chance we shall have to take. Now, we must both look into the mirror and think cockroach thoughts about Oliver Biggles.'

So they stood side by side, gazing into the mirror. Mr Surd focused on the image of a foul scuttling insect and Slugger, whose knowledge of the animal kingdom was sketchy, tried to picture a male chicken. He soon found his attention

wandering but he dared not break up the united gaze until at long last the bell rang.

'We'd better put the mirror away now, Mr Surd,' he said with a silent cheer, 'before the others come in.'

'I shall hide it among my bus magazines in the staff room,' replied the maths teacher, replacing the mirror in the paper bag. 'By the end of today, Oliver Biggles will see a cockroach in every mirror he looks in, and during tomorrow's maths lesson we'll really have some fun, eh, Stubbins?'

***

Oli's hopes that Slugger's stint as a blue-faced baboon would have left him more respectful, humble even, were quickly dashed. If anything, he seemed cockier than ever and spent most of the first lesson looking over at Oli and sniggering. Oli was mystified.

'Why isn't he scared of being cursed again?' he whispered to Skipjack.

'Perhaps he enjoyed being a baboon so much that he wants you to curse him again,' Skipjack whispered back.

The first sign of real trouble came just before break, when Slugger leaned over to Oli and muttered, 'I wouldn't use the toilets in the changing rooms if I were you. You might see something nasty in the mirror. Har-har.'

The mirror! A cold hand clutched at Oli's heart and squeezed. Slugger must have stolen the mirror and used it to curse him back! Oh, why had he left it in the tree house? Oli spent the rest of the lesson wondering what horrible creature Slugger had chosen for him and when the bell rang he raced off to find out. He avoided the changing rooms, knowing that Slugger would follow him there for a good gloat. Instead he ran down the stairs to the visitors' loo by the front door. There, behind a safely locked door, he summoned all his courage and peeped in the mirror.

His reflection was normal. Phew! Oli collapsed against the wall, but then he un-collapsed again: just because it was normal now did not mean it would *stay* normal. As long as the curse was on him he was in danger. He needed a plan. He needed Skipjack.

He found his friend at last in a corner of the playground, hiding from Katie Adams.

'She wants to kiss me to see if I'll turn into a prince,' he shuddered. 'What's up, Oli?'

'I think Slugger's stolen the mirror and put a curse on me.'

'No! What are you?'

'Nothing yet, but I won't feel safe until we've stopped him and got the mirror back.'

'I suppose now we must get him to forgive you, for changing him into a baboon,' said Skipjack.

Oli snorted. 'Can you imagine Slugger forgiving anyone for anything? It's hopeless.'

Skipjack patted him on the back. 'There'll be a way – there always is. Leave it to me.'

By home time there was still no sign of change in Oli's reflection, but this did not lessen Tara's excitement at the news that her brother might be turning into an animal of some kind.

'I hope you're a dog!' she cried. 'I'd love a dog!'

'You needn't sound so pleased about it,' grumbled Oli.

'Cheer up, matey,' said Skipjack. 'I've got a plan.'

Generally speaking, Skipjack's plans were battier than a cricket shop and such was the case with this plan.

'We're going to sneak round to Slugger's house tonight and scare him into forgiving you,' he told Oli.

'OK so far,' said Oli warily, 'but how?'

'That's the brilliant part. I'm going to dress up as a Zombie Witch Doctor, with the mask Sid gave me, and appear at his window and tell him in my spookiest voice that he's got to uncurse you or he will suffer a million gruesome deaths.'

Oli was warming to this plan. 'I could bring my old bongo drums and play them in the background, for atmosphere.'

'Can I come, too?' pleaded Tara. 'I can make a really good witch noise. Listen.' And she threw her head back in a piercing cackle.

Oli winced. 'Er, thanks but no thanks, Tara.'

His sister frowned, but she said nothing.

'We'll meet at the corner of Slugger's road and Market Street at 2 a.m. tonight,' said Skipjack. 'Get it?'

'Got it,' grinned Oli.

'Good.'

So at a quarter to two, wearing his black Secret Agent clothes and with his bongos tucked under his arm, Oli slipped out of his house and flitted through the silent streets to the corner of Slugger's road. There was no sign of Skipjack. Oli waited, trying not to feel scared as he peered through the darkness for his friend. He glanced at his watch. It was now 2.05. Perhaps Skipjack

had been caught sneaking out of his house?
Perhaps he had been stopped by a policeman?
Perhaps he had been murdered on this very spot
by an axe-wielding maniac!

A nearby rustle made Oli spin round in alarm.

A headless skeleton was rising up from behind
a bush.

Zombies and Cannibals

'Argh!' yelled Oli and took off.

'Stop!' came a shout from behind. 'It's me!'

Recognising the voice, Oli screeched to a halt and turned round. Skipjack pulled off his black balaclava and waved it at him. Oli now recognised the luminous skeleton pyjamas, too, and he felt a little foolish.

'You scared me to death!' he hissed as he retraced his steps. 'Why did you have to hide like that?'

'Because I could hardly stand around in the street looking like this, could I?' Skipjack hissed back, indicating the pyjamas. 'I wore the balaclava so I wouldn't be recognised. I thought if I was stopped I could pretend to be practising for Halloween.'

'Where's the mask?'

'Here,' said Skipjack, pulling it out of a black bin bag. Oli stared in wonder at the shrivelled hair, the hideous mouth gaping in a silent scream and the big black circles, like sunken sockets, where the eyes should have been. 'Well,' he said at last, 'if that doesn't scare Slugger, nothing will.'

As they crept towards Slugger's house, Skipjack whispered, 'We must go carefully past the front of the house, cos that's where Slugger's parents' bedroom is. Slugger's room is the only one at the back, so as long as we're not too noisy we should be fine. His window is above the back porch so you'll have to give me a leg-up.'

'How do you know so much about the inside of Slugger's house?' asked Oli.

'Because he was my best friend in nursery school,' whispered Skipjack.

Oli thought about this. 'You can't have had much choice,' he said.

'I didn't. You hadn't moved here yet.'

Skipjack put on the mask while Oli stood by the porch and made a stirrup with his hands. Skipjack was about to step into it when he paused.

'Oli, suppose my mask really does have magic powers like your mirror. If we mess about with it like this we might make something really scary happen.'

The same thought had been kicking around at the back of Oli's mind all evening but he had stubbornly ignored it; Skipjack's mask was his only hope of being de-cursed.

'I saw this film once,' continued Skipjack, 'set in Africa, and the baddie used a magic mask to wake up the living dead. But they turned out to be the living dead of cannibals and they ate him.'

'Shall I wear the mask instead and you can play the bongos?' suggested Oli.

Skipjack considered. He had spent all evening perfecting his Zombie Witch Doctor act. The risk of being eaten by living dead cannibals was surely quite small and not worth giving up such a splendid chance to frighten the spots off Slugger.

'No, thanks,' he said. 'I'll do it.'

With a hoist from Oli, Skipjack scrambled up to the porch roof, where he crouched below Slugger's window. 'Ready?' he whispered down to Oli.

'Ready,' grinned Oli with his hands poised over his bongos.

Skipjack rose until the mask and the top half of the luminous skeleton were above the sill. Then he began to knock slowly on the glass – knock, knock, knock – while Oli kept time on his bongos – boom, boom, boom.

Slugger had been tossing and turning all night, plagued with horrible dreams about killer chickens. Now the chickens had surrounded him and were pecking at his feet. Peck, peck, peck, knock, knock, knock, boom, boom, boom.

Slugger sat up in alarm, his heart thudding. He looked towards the window and froze.

Glaring in at him was the most terrifying monster he had ever seen. It had a grotesque, warpainted face with a mouth twisted into an evil grin, big black holes for eyes and a shock of white hair. And it didn't have a body! Just a skeleton. As Slugger stared, too petrified to move, the thing began to speak.

'Slugger Stubbins!' it boomed. 'I am the all-powerful Zombie Witch Doctor! I have come to warn you that if you do not release Oli Biggles from his curse you will be doomed! Doomed!'

Slugger broke out in a cold sweat of terror.

'Nod if you understand!' commanded the Zombie Witch Doctor.

Slugger gulped and nodded.

'You also must promise not to bully anyone ever again. Nod.'

Slugger nodded.

'And you must never again accuse Skipjack Haynes of doing a high tackle when he didn't. Nod.'

Slugger nodded.

'You have been wise, Slugger Stubbins. You –'
The Zombie Witch Doctor stopped. An eerie
noise had begun somewhere behind him; a
miserable moaning sound like that of an English
rugby fan watching Scotland win the Calcutta
Cup. As Skipjack listened, the moans grew
louder and higher. Oli heard them too and his
bongos fell silent, leaving the ghostly cries to fill
the air with pain and dread. What creature on

earth could be producing such gruesome howls?

'The cannibals are coming!' squeaked the Zombie Witch Doctor. 'Help!' He vanished, while the terrified Slugger dived under his bedclothes and shook like a jelly.

In his hurry to escape from the approaching cannibals, Skipjack lost his footing on the porch roof and slid off. Luckily Oli was underneath to break his fall and when they had both scrambled to their feet they sprinted like Olympic champions away from the bloodcurdling wails of the cannibals.

They did not pause for breath until they reached Oli's gate. 'I wonder if they've eaten Slugger,' puffed Skipjack.

'If so, I hope he had time to un-curse me first,' panted Oli.

'They might come for us, too,' warned Skipjack, 'cos of the mask. Barricade your bedroom door, Oli. See you in the morning, I hope.'

The luminous skeleton disappeared into the night and the secret agent crept back to his bed. As he lay awake, wondering whether he really should drag all his furniture in front of his door, he thought he heard the staircase creak. The cannibals! His heart pounding, Oli kept his eyes fixed on the door handle. But it did not turn and finally Oli began to relax. He must have imagined it.

At 7.27 precisely on Friday morning, the alarm clock beside Mr Vernon Surd's narrow iron bed began to beep. Mr Surd reached out his long bony arm and switched it off. Then he wasted three whole minutes just lying in bed and smiling to himself. Today he would turn Oliver Biggles into a cockroach in front of the whole class.

At 7.40 Mrs Stubbins marched into her son's room to pull off his blankets, but Slugger was holding onto them with an iron grip, so she shook him instead.

'Get up, Melvyn,' she ordered.

'Have they gone?' whimpered Slugger.

'Have who gone?'

'The Zombie Witch Doctor and the cannibals,' he quavered.

Mrs Stubbins clicked her tongue. 'If this is just another excuse not to go to school then I warn you, Melvyn Stubbins –'

'It's not an excuse! The Zombie Witch Doctor came in the night and then the cannibals came and even the Zombie Witch Doctor was scared of them and he's all-powerful!'

'If you're not out of that bed and downstairs in three minutes, I'll show you all-powerful,' said his mother grimly.

At 7.45 Tara popped her head round her brother's door.

'How did it go last night?' she demanded without preamble.

Oli surfaced and blinked. A strange dark blur was swimming about in his doorway and before his very eyes it slowly took the form of his sister, tapping her foot impatiently. 'Hi, T,' he mumbled.

'What happened last night?' repeated Tara.

Oli frowned. 'It was all going brilliantly but then something really weird happened: we heard these wailing, moaning sounds, like cannibals.'

Tara frowned. 'Cannibals?'

Oli nodded. 'That's what Skipjack said they were. Anyway, they were massively spooky, so we ran away. I won't know if the Slugger Plan worked till we get to school. I only hope the cannibals didn't eat him too quickly.'

'Cannibals,' repeated Tara to herself as she went downstairs. 'Strange.'

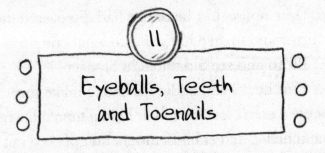

11
Eyeballs, Teeth and Toenails

It did not take Slugger Stubbins long to decide that, terrifying though his nocturnal visitors were, even more terrifying was his own mother. He had better get up. Also, if he didn't get up, he wouldn't be able to un-curse Oli and then he would be doomed.

But how exactly did you un-curse someone? It now occurred to Slugger that the Zombie Witch Doctor had legged it from the cannibals before giving him any tips on this very important point. Oli himself would know, of course, but Slugger would rather have faced the combined horrors of the Zombie Witch Doctor and the cannibals *and* his mother all together than ask Oli.

Then he remembered a snippet of conversation he had overheard while spying on Oli, Skipjack and Tara from the bushes below the tree house, just before he had discovered the mirror and turned himself into a baboon.

I'll go and see Sid, thought Slugger.

First he peeked under his bed to make sure there weren't any cannibals hiding there. Then he scurried across his bedroom and peeked out of the window to make sure the garden was also cannibal-free. Then he checked the street and the neighbours' gardens from all the other upstairs windows. Then he got up, dressed and went downstairs.

'I gotta run, Mum,' he called from the hall. 'I gotta see someone before school.'

The frowning head of Mrs Stubbins appeared round the kitchen door. 'Not another detention?'

''Course not!' Slugger looked offended.

'What about breakfast?'

'I'll stop at the sweet shop. Bye, Mum.'

Slugger approached Mrs Happy's Pizza Shop with all the enthusiasm of a pirate approaching the end of the plank, with Sid playing the role of the circling shark. He dreaded confessing that he had put a curse on her friend. Luckily, however much she would want to chew him up and spit

him out, she would have to help him to help Oli.
So Slugger took a deep breath and rang the door
bell.

He saw Sid come into the shop from the back,
look across to the glass front door and stop in
surprise. Then she came forward and unlocked
the door.

'It's too early for an egg and bacon pizza,' she
told him.

'I've come to talk about Oli Biggles,' mumbled
Slugger.

Sid's eyes narrowed. 'You'd better come in.'

Once he was perched uncertainly on a stool
at the pizza bar, she demanded, 'So, what about
Oli?'

'Mr Surd put a curse on Oli,' mumbled
Slugger, 'and he wants to know how to take it off
again.'

Sid watched him carefully. 'Why did he send
you?' she asked.

'He was too scared to come himself,' Slugger
said, without looking at her.

'And why does he want to take the curse off
again?'

'He was visited in the night by the Zombie Witch Doctor,' explained Slugger.

'The who?'

'The Zombie Witch Doctor.'

'I think Mr Surd has been telling you stories.'

'It's true!' insisted Slugger, looking at her for the first time. 'He appeared at my – at Mr Surd's window, and he had a horrible face with warpaint and his eyes were missing.'

This Zombie Witch Doctor was beginning to sound familiar. 'Did he by any chance have white hair and a bad case of tooth decay?' asked Sid.

Slugger nodded. 'That's right!'

Sid shook her head gravely. 'You did the right thing coming to me,' she told him. 'He is an immensely powerful and dangerous magic man.'

Her words confirmed Slugger's darkest fears. 'Please help me!' he wailed.

'First of all you must tell me exactly what you and Mr Surd did,' said Sid.

Slugger reddened. 'I didn't want to do it. Mr Surd made me,' he mumbled.

'Made you do what?'

'Made me help him put a curse on Oli with

the magic mirror. Mr Surd wants to smash
the mirror in maths today and turn Oli into a
cockroach.'

Sid fought down her urge to grab Slugger by
the collar, drag him into the kitchen and feed
him into her dough-making machine. 'In that
case I'm not surprised the Zombie Witch Doctor
is after you,' she said.

Slugger hung his head. 'He said if I don't un-
curse Oli I'll be doomed. But he didn't tell me
how to do it.'

'Luckily, it's so simple that even you can do it,

Slugger. All you have to do is to forgive him for cursing you.'

Slugger frowned. 'How do I forgive him?' he asked.

'You just have to stop being angry and think forgiving thoughts,' she explained. 'Just say, "I forgive Oli, I forgive Oli" lots of times. Go on, try it now. '

For a few moments the air was heavy with concentration as Slugger clenched his fists and frowned hard. Sid watched him, fascinated by how much effort he had to put into something as simple as thinking forgiving thoughts. Finally Slugger's face cleared and he looked up at her.

'I think I've done it,' he said.

'Congratulations. Now you just have to persuade Mr Surd to do the same.'

She was still watching Slugger closely and the gleam that now came into his eye was easy to read. It was a gleam that said, 'Now that I'm safe, it doesn't matter whether Mr Surd turns Oli into a cockroach or not.'

'Because if you don't get Mr Surd to take off the curse,' she continued casually, 'you will still be responsible for half of anything that happens to Oli, so you will still be doomed. And believe me, Slugger, when the Zombie Witch Doctor says "doomed", he means doomed. When I was in Africa, a boy was buried alive in a coffin full of scorpions by the Zombie Witch Doctor. Another one disappeared completely and all they ever found was his eyeballs in a bag with his teeth and his toenail clippings. They think the rest of him was eaten by cannibals.'

Slugger gasped. 'They were there last night, too!'

'There you go.' She leaned forward and peered at Slugger.

'What are you doing?' he asked, drawing back in alarm.

'Just checking what colour your eyes are, so I can help to recognise them when they are found in a bag. You might be hard to identify by your toenail clippings.' Sid went to the door and opened it. 'Goodbye, Slugger,' she said.

'Here he comes!' cried Oli.

Skipjack joined him at the window of the

empty classroom and looked out at the bulky figure of Slugger hurrying across the school car park.

'He looks nice and frightened,' he remarked.

'Come on,' said Oli.

They crept to the door of the classroom and listened. They soon heard quick, heavy footsteps go past. Skipjack grinned. 'That's our Slugger,' he said. They opened the door a fraction and peeped out.

Slugger was now standing outside the staff-room door further along the corridor, exactly as they had expected. After a moment or two Mr Surd emerged from the staff room and the pair stepped away from the door. Slugger began to talk in a very animated way, waving his arms about and pulling dreadful faces, much to Skipjack's delight.

'He makes a brilliant Zombie,' he giggled.

'Mr Surd doesn't look very impressed,' whispered Oli.

'You can never tell with old Vernon,' Skipjack pointed out. 'Years of maths have frozen his face.'

Soon Mr Surd withdrew into the staff room and Slugger, after staying to frown at the space where the maths teacher had been, turned away down the corridor.

'I think it's time we had a little chat with baboon-boy,' said Oli. 'Follow me.'

They found Slugger in their own classroom, hovering anxiously near the window. He shrank back when he saw Oli and Skipjack approaching.

'Mr Surd made me do it and now I can't get him to stop. It's not my fault any more if you turn into a cockroach. The Zombie Witch Doctor is going to blame me and it's not fair.' The words came tumbling out in a rush.

'A cockroach,' repeated Oli. 'Is that the curse?'

Slugger nodded. 'He's going to smash the mirror in maths. And then stamp on you.'

Oli gulped.

'But that's murder!' cried Skipjack.

Slugger nodded. 'That's why the Zombie Witch Doctor will be after us. I tried to tell Mr Surd but he didn't believe me. And now we're both doomed. It's not fair.'

'Not fair?' cried Skipjack. 'You deserve

everything you get! I hope the Zombie Witch Doctor boils you alive!'

In his fury Skipjack had forgotten that he *was* the Zombie Witch Doctor.

'There's still a chance that his curse hasn't worked,' said Oli. 'I keep checking my reflection and I don't look any different. Perhaps now that the mirror's cracked it doesn't work properly any more. But we still need to come up with a plan, just in case. Skip?'

Skipjack put his brain (the eighth wonder of the world) into action. 'We have to get the mirror back,' he said. 'When Mr Surd brings it to the classroom you must create a diversion, Oli, so I can grab it and run away.'

'Good idea,' agreed Oli. 'But you must be

careful not to smash it. And we should have a Plan B just in case.'

'Here's Plan B,' announced Skipjack and he produced from his pocket an empty matchbox.

Oli looked puzzled. 'How is that Plan B?'

'If he does turn you into a cockroach,' explained Skipjack, 'I'll pop you in here before he can stamp on you.'

'You'll never fit a cockroach in there,' objected Slugger. 'You'd never even get a female chicken in there, and cockroaches are much bigger.'

'Slugger,' sighed Skipjack. 'You are awesomely thick. Now, your job is to rugby-tackle Mr Surd if he goes anywhere near that mirror, OK?'

Slugger nodded. This he understood.

Showdown with Mr Surd

Oli and Skipjack were not alone in trying to stop Vernon Surd's evil plan. Back in Mrs Happy's Pizza Shop, Sid had no faith in Slugger's ability to persuade Mr Surd of the dangers of the Zombie Witch Doctor and she was busy planning her own way to convince him. First she went upstairs and changed into an old set of paint-splattered overalls. Then she found some brushes and paint pots and a large bucket. Then she called the school.

'Hiya, this is Mrs Biggles. I'm afraid Oli left his maths books at home. Can you tell me when he has maths, please? Lesson 2, at 10 o'clock. Oh, dear, I'll only just manage that. If you could tell me which room he'll be in, then if I'm late I can take the books straight there. Room 15. Where exactly is that? On the first floor at the western end. Thank you so much. Goodbye.'

Then she went round to Skipjack's house.

At about five to ten, Tara was in her history
class, concealed behind The Big Book of Vikings
and frowning at the fortune-telling bones on her
desk. She had been secretly casting her bones all
morning and they kept falling in the same shape
– a big 'O'. Tara just knew it was a warning and
she also knew the warning was for Oli. But what
should she do? She glanced absently out of the
window and then she sat up. Striding across the
car park, laden with pots and buckets and a long
wooden ladder, was Sid.

Tara swept the bones back into their bag and
her hand shot up. 'Can I be excused, please?' she
called. Barely waiting for the teacher's nod, she
was out of her seat, out of her classroom, and
speeding along the corridor to the front door.

She was just in time to see the end of Sid's
ladder disappearing round the side of the school.
Tara raced after her but when she rounded the
corner she screeched to a halt.

Sid was propping up her ladder right outside

135

the headmaster's window.

'Sid!' hissed Tara, and Sid turned round. When she saw Tara she grinned and came back to the corner.

'Hiya, Tara! What are you doing here?'

'More to the point, what are *you* doing *there*?' hissed Tara. 'That's the headmaster's office.'

'Really? Lucky I'm wearing this disguise. I've come to scare the hair off Mr Surd with Skipjack's Death Mask.'

Tara's eyes lit up. 'Can I make spooky noises in the background?'

'Smashing,' chuckled Sid. 'You wait here. I'm going to climb up my ladder and listen below the window and when I hear Mr Surd's voice I'll begin. Then you can start being spooky.'

'OK,' agreed Tara, just as the 10 o'clock bell started to ring.

Mr Surd returned to the staff room at the end of Lesson 1 to collect the mirror. He was feeling strangely calm, as if he were floating far above the bustle and stress of the school. He was on the verge of fulfilling his destiny as the Ultimate

136

Force of Discipline. Oliver Biggles had come to represent in his mind the generations of children who had plagued his teaching career with their stupidity and laziness. These monsters had transformed him from a bright-eyed youngster, keen to spread the joys of mathematics, into a bitter and miserable old man. Turning Biggles into a cockroach would be revenge on them all. With the mirror tucked under one arm, Mr Surd set off for his moment of glory.

'He's coming!' called Skipjack from the door of Room 15. 'Don't forget, Oli, keep as far away from him as possible. That way, if the worst comes to the worst, we'll have time to put Plan B into action.' He patted his pocket, in which nestled the empty matchbox. 'Slugger, you must sit right at the front next to me, so you can tackle him. Sorry, Ned, but you'll have to move. Mr Surd is planning to be very mean to Oli today and Slugger's going to help us stop him, so he needs to sit here.'

Skipjack's arm-waving directions were cut short by the entry of Mr Surd. The class fell quiet. The lesson had begun.

Directly below Room 15, the headmaster was sitting at his desk trying to write reports when he heard clattering sounds from outside. He glanced round to the window. A large person in overalls was just about to climb a ladder and, judging by the collection of paint pots and brushes at her feet, this person was a painter. The painter saw him, smiled cheerfully and waved. The headmaster returned both the cheerful smile and the wave. How nice to have such happy workmen about the place, he thought and he rose with relief from his reports and went over to the window for a chat.

Oli's heart was pounding like a pneumatic drill as he watched Mr Surd limp to the table at the front of the class. The silent room echoed to the sound of the unbalanced teacher's footsteps. Mr Sud set down a stack of books and papers, on top of which was something wrapped in brown paper – the mirror!

Then his cold eye swept the class and he saw that Slugger was sitting right at the front, next to the lunatic Haynes boy. He guessed that Stubbins had confessed his part in the cockroach scheme to Biggles and his crazy friend, and was now on their side. But their resistance was pointless – he had the power to triumph over them all.

He cleared his throat and picked up his pointed stick. 'I have the results of Tuesday's fractions test,' he announced in his Dalek voice. 'They are, with the usual single exception, a disaster.' He turned to Oli. 'Yours was by far the worst, Biggles. What do you have to say to that?'

Oli had nothing at all to say to that – he

was too busy trying to think up a diversion so that Skipjack could grab the mirror. Mr Surd began to tap the table with his stick. 'Shall I tell everyone what you got?' he said.

'Could you come and whisper it to me instead?' asked Oli, hoping to lure him away from the table. The class laughed.

Mr Surd nearly took the mirror out and smashed it there and then, but he fought down the urge. He was not going to rush his moment of revenge. Instead he took a few steps towards Oli, intending to vent his anger by whacking his stick on the boy's desk. But a slight movement from Skipjack made him turn and hurry back to the front of the class, where he whacked his own table instead.

'Come and sit here at the front, Biggles,' he hissed. 'Stubbins, swap places with him.'

Oli gulped. Would Slugger have the brainpower to cope with this unexpected move?

Luckily, fear of the Zombie Witch Doctor had given Slugger a primitive survival instinct that didn't depend on brainpower. 'I can't, sir,' he said.

Vernon Surd whacked the table again. 'Do as I say!' he yelled.

At the foot of her ladder, Sid was still locked in chat with the headmaster. She could hear Mr Surd yelling and whacking and was beginning to despair of getting up her ladder in time to help Oli.

'I can't move, Mr Surd,' insisted Slugger. 'I'm stuck to my seat – look.' And, holding onto the seat of his chair, he jiggled up and down. 'Someone must have put glue on it.'

The class laughed again.

Mr Surd stamped his foot. 'Shut up!' he shouted. 'Shut up, all of you!' He was trembling with rage as he glared round the room. 'You sit there, the lot of you, more foolish than a flock of sheep and too stupid to do anything but giggle – "tee, hee, hee". If only you knew of my powers you would have more respect. If only you knew what I could do to every single one of you, just by the strength of my mind.'

The children looked at one another, all thinking the same thing: Mr Surd has gone mad.

'You don't believe me, do you?' demanded

Vernon Surd. 'You doubt my powers. Ha! I shall show you! I shall turn Oliver Biggles into a –'

He stopped. His gaze was fixed on the window at the back of the classroom. Seeing his eyes widen with disbelief, the children twisted round in their seats and gasped.

At the window was a grotesque face. Its skin was shrivelled and brown and streaked with warpaint, hollow black sockets were all that was left of its eyes and its gaping mouth was studded with rotten teeth. Its hair was bone-white and stuck out in random tufts. It was . . .

'The Zombie Witch Doctor!' yelled Slugger.

'The Zombie Witch Doctor?' echoed the rest of the class, thrilled. Oli and Skipjack exchanged glances. How had that got there?

Then the awful face began to speak.

'Vernon Surd!' boomed Sid. 'You are an evil man!' She longed to point an accusing finger at him but she dared not reveal the painting overalls. Instead she repeated, 'Evil! Evil!' in a rising yodel. Room 15 sat rooted to their chairs with excitement (all except Katie Adams, who slid quietly to the floor in a faint).

In the office below, the headmaster, who had at last returned to his reports, reflected that although it was nice to have such cheerful workmen, they should be asked to sing more quietly.

Meanwhile Sid's voice was the cue for her assistant to start the spooky noises.

'Ooooooh, Ahhhhhhhh, Eeeeeeeeee!' howled Tara from behind her corner of the building.

'The cannibals!' shouted Oli, Skipjack and Slugger together.

'Cannibals?' echoed the rest of the class, even more thrilled. This was all so much better than maths.

'It's nonsense!' shouted Mr Surd over the babble. He had to regain control. His moment of triumph was in serious danger of being lost forever.

'Reverse the curse,' boomed Sid, 'or you will be DOOMED!'

'*Please* reverse the curse, Mr Surd,' begged Slugger, 'or I'll be doomed with you!'

'We're all doomed!' shouted someone. This was an idea which caught on fast and soon the whole class was out of their seats and running around, shouting, 'We're all doomed!'

'Silence!' screamed Vernon Surd.

'Obey the Zombie Witch Doctor!' boomed Sid. 'You must forgive Oli, because he is a smashing boy!'

Oli and Skipjack exchanged more glances. So that was it: any Zombie Witch Doctor who used the word 'smashing' had to have Sid hiding underneath. But this did not explain the cannibals, who continued to wail horribly in the background.

'Obey the Zombie Witch Doctor, Mr Surd!' shouted the class, thoroughly enjoying themselves.

'Silence!' he screamed back. 'There is no such thing as a Zombie Witch Doctor!' And he grabbed the mirror and limped at top speed to the window.

Sid saw him coming and nearly fell off her ladder in her haste to slither to the ground. While Mr Surd fumbled with the window catch, Tara shot out to help Sid pick up her props and together they scampered away around the corner of the building, just as the window was pushed wide open.

'See?' Vernon Surd demanded to the class. 'There is no one there.'

'That means he's made himself invisible!' cried Oli, keen to keep the chaos going. 'He's probably come into this very room!'

Skipjack joined in the general squealing that greeted this announcement but then he stopped. He had seen that Mr Surd was holding the mirror. Skipjack's heart lurched. How could he get it without smashing it? Now Mr Surd was staring hard at Oli; there was no time to lose. Skipjack began to creep forwards.

But although Mr Surd was staring at Oli, he wasn't seeing Oli, he was seeing a giant cockroach. He blinked hard and stared again. He still saw a cockroach. This isn't possible, he thought, I haven't smashed the mirror yet.

'We're all doomed!' shouted another voice happily. Mr Surd turned round and saw another enormous cockroach. And then another, creeping towards him. The whole classroom was seething with huge, noisy, scuttling insects.

'Silence!' he screamed. 'Get back to your
seats!' His head was whirling. Had he turned
all the children into cockroaches? It was a
nightmare. Something flipped inside Mr Surd.
He raised the mirror high above his head and
with a cry of anguish he flung it to the floor.

There was a blinding flash of light. The
children stopped running around and stared in
the greatest astonishment. Mr Surd had turned
into a vulture. In the corner of the room, Oli felt
himself all over, but he was still Oli. Mr Surd's

spell had backfired. For a moment everything was still. Then the great black bird flapped up onto the window sill, spread its huge wings and took off.

The whole class ran to the window to watch the vulture as it circled higher and higher. In the car park below, Sid and Tara also watched, until it was just a dot in the sky.

And Mr Surd looked down at the school as it grew smaller and smaller until it was just a dot on the ground. Then he flew away to the hills, to peace.

Loose Ends

Note left on Oli's pillow that night:

Warning:

If you don't clean up the tree house TOMORROW and find a NEW ZOO for Tara, we will come and EAT you.
From

The Cannibals.

Conversation between Oli and Ned Trotter in the playground the following morning.

> Ned: *G-guess what, Oli? I'm going to make sure I never get bullied again: I am going to become a Human Weapon.*

Oli (surprised): *That's good, Ned. How?*

Ned: *Remember that c-competition in the c-computer magazine Slugger tore up?*

Oli: *Of course, Ned. Don't tell me you won?*

Ned: *I did win. I won five hundred pounds!*

Oli: *Wow, Ned. What are you going to spend it on?*

Ned: *K-K . . .*

Oli (groaning): *Not computer stuff, Ned, please.*

Ned: *No, Oli – K-Karate lessons!*

Letter received by Tara the next afternoon, on Zoo paper:

Dear Miss Biggles,

  All of us here so enjoyed your imaginative letter offering to sell your baboon to the zoo. I wonder if you bought it from our shop here — they are very realistic, aren't they?

  By a strange coincidence, our own pair of (real!) baboons has

just had a baby! We all loved
the name you gave to your toy
baboon, so we are going to call
this new arrival Slugger!

Here is a free family ticket
to the zoo. I hope that you will
come and see Slugger very soon.

Yours sincerely,

Annie Malinstinct
Zoo Director

Article in the local newspaper, 3 weeks later:

Surd Mystery Continues

As the search continues for vanished
school teacher Mr Vernon Surd, a
mystery is unfolding at the local bus
station, where this keen bus-watcher
spent so many happy hours.

A strange black bird, which witnesses
describe as a kind of vulture, has been
regularly spotted sitting in the exact spot

on the footbridge where Mr Surd used to stand to watch the buses. While police express doubts of finding the missing maths teacher alive, bus driver Mr Albert Grimble claims the vulture is the spirit of his vanished friend. 'This bus station was like a second home to him,' says Mr Grimble. 'I'm not at all surprised that this is where he has chosen to spend his Afterlife.'